SENTINEL

THE VIGILANTE CHRONICLES™ BOOK TWO

NATALIE GREY
MICHAEL ANDERLE

DISRUPTIVE IMAGINATION®

Sentinel (this book) is a work of fiction.

All of the characters, organizations, and events portrayed in this novel are either products of the author's imagination or are used fictitiously. Sometimes both.

LMBPN Publishing
PMB 196, 2540 South Maryland Pkwy
Las Vegas, NV 89109

First US edition, June 2018
Version 1.01, June 2018

SENTINEL TEAM

Thanks to the JIT Readers

James Caplan
Mary Morris
Kelly O'Donnell
John Raisor
John Ashmore
Peter Manis
Larry Omans
Paul Westman
Micky Cocker

If We've missed anyone, please let us know!

Editor
Lynne Stiegler

From Natalie

For M and T

From Michael

To Family, Friends and
Those Who Love
To Read.
May We All Enjoy Grace
To Live The Life We Are
Called.

"That is my offer. Take it or leave it." The hooded figure in the video frame steepled his fingers and leaned back.

Torcellan, and male. Beyond that Rald could not tell anything about this person, up to and including how the male had known to contact him. Rald didn't like that on principle. He was Shrillexian, and an offer of vengeance promised violence with a purpose.

He couldn't ask for more on that front, but he didn't like not knowing the people who gave him information—not when his entire operation hinged on that information. *Especially* when it was information he should have had to pay for. There were clearly strings attached.

He flexed and clenched his fingers. Three weeks ago, an old friend on Devon had called in his allies. Years ago they had been in business together, had flown on the same ship —even managed to be co-captains without too many problems. It had been a great partnership—until Jutkelon had signed on with a mercenary syndicate.

Rald had decided to remain on his own, but Jutkelon got a steadier stream of contracts through the syndicate. He had funds saved for when he decided to build his base on Devon—but in return, he had to pay part of his take to the syndicate.

Rald had never gone for that sort of thing. *No one* told him what to do.

Still, he didn't bear Jutkelon any ill will. They even saw each other occasionally, since Rald's team often took contracts to guard the transit and cargo ships traveling to and from the planet.

Rald had been out of contact on an urgent mission when Jutkelon had sent out the call for backup. He'd sent a message back as soon as he'd seen Jutkelon's and received only silence in return.

He had begrudgingly contacted the syndicate to get the details. Three fully-crewed, fully-armed ships had been sent to take down someone who was meddling in their business.

They'd failed miserably.

Jutkelon was dead, those three ships had never come back, and when Rald had asked around to see why, all anyone would tell him was that the planet Devon was forbidden. Further questioning had uncovered that Devon had been renamed 'High Tortuga' and that it was now under the control of Queen Bethany Anne, formerly of the Etheric Empire.

Like *hell* it did. Who did they think they were? They had come out of nowhere, these humans, flashing tech that was too good to be true, and started flinging rules around as though they owned the galaxy.

High Tortuga—like they could just rename an entire planet!

Rald didn't really care if the humans wanted to dress up in fancy clothes and call themselves kings. Hell, if their money was good enough and they offered enough fights, he'd sign right up and call them "Your Supreme Majesty" or whatever they wanted. Rich people got weird after a while but they were the ones who kept him in food and fights, so he had learned to let the weirdness go.

It was the way of the world, after all. If you were strong enough, you took what you wanted. Rald helped people who did that, and if *he* didn't, someone else would. There was no use complaining about it.

But now these humans were turning the established order on its head. They hadn't taken over the businesses completely, but instead had laid down the law with the owners and told them what they could and couldn't do.

Rald didn't care for that, *especially* when they just went and killed the people who didn't comply.

So he'd made himself a promise to find whoever had done that to Jutkelon and make them hurt. He'd asked around at the syndicate, but no one seemed to know anything—until this mysterious Torcellan had called out of the blue and offered information.

All Rald had to do was break his only rule and join something called the 'Yennai Corporation.' He'd pay the share of his take and pass along information, and in return they would give him any information they found on the human who had killed Jutkelon and their ships would back him up if he cornered the bastard. As a gesture of goodwill, they had even given Rald a possible name for the human's ship—*Shinigami.* The information was unconfirmed, but it was more than Rald had been able to find on his own.

Take it or leave it.

He'd take it, Rald decided. He had to. Jutkelon had asked for his help but he hadn't come through…and now Jutkelon was dead. Some son of a Hieten had gone in there and murdered his friend, and Rald owed it to him to return the favor.

He could figure out who the Torcellan was later. In the meantime, he was going to get even with whoever had done this—but if they'd taken out three ships he was going to need the corporation's help, as much as he hated to admit it.

He nodded at the figure on the screen. "I'll take it. I'll be in contact when I get to Devon."

"Ah. For that, you will need my help. Ships must be cleared to land there." Rald got the impression the Torcellan was smiling. "There is a berth for you on the merchant ship *Ulys.* You'll be registered as a worker on the ship. I've sent the itinerary. Meet it at Gammon."

The screen winked off and Rald frowned. He read the instructions that had just come through and frowned harder. No weaponry? This had to be a fucking joke.

Rald wasn't laughing, and by the time he was done with the humans they wouldn't be either. As far as he was concerned, anyone and everyone who'd had anything to do with Jutkelon's death was fair game.

Carter wiped his hands on a dishtowel and backed out of

the kitchen at Aebura's as he called instructions to Oemuga, his new assistant.

"And make sure they don't shortchange you on the fruit!" The last piece of advice was probably lost in the clatter of cooking and juice-pressing.

He shook his head. Oemuga was a good assistant, but he needed to get better at bargaining. Ubuara always looked for accord when they were making deals, which meant they were likely to compromise too much. The same was true of the Ubuara he was training to be bartenders.

He'd have to ask Aebura how she'd learned to be so shrewd in business. Maybe she could teach Oemuga and the others. She'd left Tethra a few weeks ago after signing over her bar to Carter so she could work in the newly-liberated mining town.

Carter whistled, his spirits lifting at the thought of being able to talk to her again. Aebura always cheered him up. She had such a simple, happy outlook on life: gathering friends together was good, and worrying about the future was bad. She also had a sense of humor that always startled him, and he was grateful to count her amongst his friends.

He was over by the bar getting himself a cup of water when he noticed one of the patrons and stopped dead. "Barnabas! I thought you'd left."

"I was going to," Barnabas told him. "But then I figured I'd get one last glass of juice." He held up his glass with a mournful look. "We haven't been able to synthesize it yet."

"And I," a young woman with black hair interrupted, "came here expecting to find him doing drugs, and found out that 'juice' actually means *juice*."

"Carter, may I introduce Tabitha?" Barnabas requested

politely. "Tabitha, Carter runs this bar. He helped us against the mine owner a few weeks back. Carter, Tabitha is—"

"*Ranger Two.*" Carter breathed. He had to work to keep from gawping like a fish, and judging by Tabitha's expression he wasn't doing too well.

"I *knew* this new armor looked good." She snickered. "It really makes my ass look—"

"He's impressed by your record of service to Bethany Anne," Barnabas told her in a pained tone. "He can't *see* your... You know what, never mind." To Carter he added, "Also, we really *do* need to find a different term. We aren't 'Ranger One' and 'Ranger Two' anymore."

"Details." Tabitha waved her hand to dismiss the problem of a name and downed the last of her Coke. "You know what this place needs? Burgers."

"We're working on that, actually." Carter grabbed a menu. "Now, if you want just some random fried stuff— fries, cheese curds...."

"Cheese curds?"

"I grew up in the Midwest. Trust me, they're good. We're still waiting on artificial production for the beef, though, so no burgers worth eating yet. We do have this kind of sausage sandwich thing."

"Like *choripan*?" Tabitha demanded. When she saw Carter's confused look, she flapped a hand. "Never mind. Bring me one, though."

"You're not being very polite," Barnabas chided.

"There's no time to be polite. I'm hungry."

"So help me, if you are rude to people here, I will *not* take you anywhere else." Barnabas glared at her.

"Fine." Tabitha threw a look at Barnabas. She turned back to Carter with her hands clasped in front of her, and her head tilted to the side. "Can you *please* bring me a sausage sandwich? I'm so hungry. I've been craving *choripan* for years because I stupidly forgot to steal a street cart as we left Earth. And a vendor."

She turned back to Barnabas. "There, was *that* polite enough to get me fed?"

Barnabas sighed and touched a hand to his forehead to rub the spot where the headache Tabitha gave him always began.

Carter grinned as soon as his back was to the Rangers. He pushed the door open into the kitchen and shouted Tabitha's order to the cook. Qiliax had come here to help after the mines were freed. Like most of the former guards there, she was a Brakalon. She barely fit in the kitchen, spending most of her day hunched over, but her food was fantastic.

She was such a good cook that he couldn't figure out why she'd ever been a guard, but she only shrugged when he asked and told him that no one hired a Brakalon for anything except hitting things very hard. Apparently, Carter was the first one who hadn't laughed at her when she'd asked him if she could try out as his cook.

Their loss, Carter's gain.

Between her cooking and Aebura's established group of regulars business was humming along, although he joked with Barnabas that half their profit margin so far was Barnabas' insane consumption of hakoj juice.

"I'll have a crate of juice ready for you by the time you leave," he told Barnabas when he got back to the front. "If you're going off to save the universe you really should have refreshments on board."

"Just make sure you don't give me any of that spoiled batch of Coke," Barnabas teased Carter wickedly. "It was really tragic," he told Tabitha. "He came here with this plan to run a bar, and he'd handle producing Coke, right? Well, his first batch just went *way* wrong. I think it's something about the water here. Anyway, he's figured out the filtration now and everything's better."

Barnabas took one look at Carter's deer-in-the-headlights expression and snorted. He was well aware that Carter had been producing Pepsi on the sly, and there was nothing he liked more than teasing Carter about it.

Tabitha looked back and forth between them, but a few seconds later the sandwich appeared in the little window next to the bar and all her attention turned to the food.

"Ohhhh, that smells so good." She grinned at Carter when he handed it over. She snatched it up and took a bite before the plate had even hit the bar. "Thankff. Oh man, thif *taftef* fo good."

"Don't talk with your mouth full," Barnabas told her.

"Wha, la vif?

Barnabas dropped his head into his hands in defeat and Carter tried to stifle his snort of laughter. "So, where's Gar?" he asked to distract Barnabas before he brought up Carter's Coke snafu again.

"Ah." Barnabas looked up again. He was studiously avoiding the sight of Tabitha eating. She was clearly playing up all the smacking sounds, looking over at him with a grin every couple of bites. "He's on the ship, getting prepared for upgrades."

"Upgrades?"

"Povvoc," Tabitha clarified around a mouthful of sandwich.

"What?"

"*Pod-doc.*" Barnabas looked like he was going to have an aneurysm. "She said 'Pod-doc.' They allow for certain changes to physiology. Now, he hasn't yet been cleared for those changes—"

"Why not?"

"For one thing, Shinigami has to learn more about his species before she just starts changing things around. There wasn't much about Luvendi in our databases. She's working with TOM to figure out what sort of upgrades would even be useful and make sure we don't mess anything up, especially in terms of cognition. Physical issues are pretty easily fixed, but once the mind goes..." Barnabas gave Carter a meaningful look. "But part of it is certainly that he hasn't fully proven himself to me. Before I allow him to take advantage of some of the best of our technology, I want to make sure he's not going to have another change of heart once he has the power the upgrades will give him."

Carter nodded in approval. Gar had helped immensely when Barnabas liberated the mines. In fact, Gar had willingly sacrificed himself to kill Lan, his former employer. The fact that he hadn't died was entirely due to the advanced tech available on the *Shinigami*.

Still, before he had come over to the side of Justice Gar had done some terrible things under Lan's orders. It made good sense to Carter that Barnabas wanted to keep an eye on Gar for a bit longer before making him any more dangerous.

Tabitha, meanwhile, finished licking off her fingers and smacked her lips. "That was amazing. I'm going to be back. Probably every day. You know what? Just have a sandwich waiting for me around this time. I'll keep a tab open."

"Are you planning to break mid-mission each day to come get a sandwich?" Barnabas inquired. He looked like he was trying not to laugh.

"I think I could get Bethany Anne to go for that. She appreciates the important things in life."

"She does," Barnabas agreed. "Honor, duty, Justice…and sandwiches, apparently."

Tabitha nodded seriously as she wiped her fingers on her napkin and threw it onto the empty plate before getting up. "Bye, Big B." She waved cheerfully to Carter, planted a kiss on Barnabas' cheek—he only sighed at this—and disappeared into the street, a surprisingly short figure all in black.

Barnabas smiled at Carter's expression. "Not what you expected from Ranger Two?"

Carter held a hand up at head height. "I thought…you know, *taller*? And serious, maybe. I mean, she's done some insane shit if even half of the stories are true. Sorry for swearing," he added hastily.

Barnabas only chuckled. "She definitely has done some…well, *impressive* things, shall we say. You could not ask for a more loyal ally. Of course, she embodies the term 'chaotic neutral.' But I've come to appreciate that chaos over the years, even if she is a bad influence on Shinigami. Probably on me, too." He set down his glass with a sigh.

"Say hello to Elisa and the kids for me. And if you ever need help, do feel free to call on either Tabitha or me. I'll be back when I can."

"Where are you going?" Carter asked curiously. He had known for a while that Barnabas intended to head off-planet, but so far he hadn't told Carter anything about where or why.

"I'm not exactly sure." Barnabas flashed Carter a smile full of teeth that were a lot sharper than humans usually had. "I'll be on the lookout for the people who came to Lan's aid. There are a lot of people out there who target planets like High Tortuga because they think no one's protecting them. My mission has always been to make people like that...reconsider their course of action."

Carter considered pointing out that people had to be alive in order to reconsider things, but decided not to say anything at all. He waved as Barnabas disappeared, then he cleaned the glass with a shake of his head.

Barnabas had been a stalwart ally and a good friend, and he was surprisingly indulgent with Carter's twins, Alanna and Samuel.

But Carter would never, *ever* want to get on his bad side.

On the *Shinigami*, Gar opened his eyes as the Pod-doc hissed open. He sat up, squinting in the bright lights. His head ached fiercely.

"Any progress?"

"Yes." Shinigami's voice came from the speakers nearby.

"Your physiology is quite interesting. Not only are your bones more brittle than those of other species, your skeletal structure is not well suited to walking on land. It supports the theory that the Luvendi did indeed evolve from marine mammals, even if it wasn't on Luvendan."

Gar nodded as he got dressed. The history of the Luvendi was shrouded in mystery. His people now lived in submerged towers in the oceans that covered the planet Luvendan, but no one could remember how and when the towers had been built.

It was a mystery that quite intrigued Shinigami.

"Barnabas is back," Shinigami reported. "He asks that you join him in the planning room."

"Of course." Gar felt the usual thrill of worry he got when he anticipated seeing Barnabas, although he was aware that he was in no danger as long as he did not do anything immoral or unjust. He was even more aware of the fact that Barnabas had very high standards

And that he was very, *very* dangerous.

Since Barnabas was back now, Gar assumed he had picked a place for them to go first in their search for Lan's allies. He adjusted his robes as he walked down the hallways, and found himself shaking his head.

Those poor bastards had no idea what was coming.

2

B arnabas waited in the planning room. True to form, he was making notes in pen on the printouts of the maps and schematics that he'd gathered for their mission. The pen was a concession he had made to Shinigami when he had pulled out a pencil and she had asked why he wanted her to have to filter graphite particles and sawdust out of the air.

He preferred to do things with paper rather than on computer screens. Something about writing and drawing cleared his mind, perhaps a legacy of his days spent among the painstakingly illuminated handwritten texts in the monastery.

It amused everyone else to poke fun at it.

When Gar came into the room Barnabas looked up with interest. The Luvendi seemed more subdued than usual, but he offered no reason for this so Barnabas decided to let it be for the moment. Gar had certainly had serious and unpleasant things to consider while he atoned for his past actions, and Barnabas believed that moral wrestling bouts were best done on one's own. He would only step in if he were asked to do so or if he sensed a problem.

"We have our first stop," Barnabas told the Luvendi. He tapped on a star chart and pulled out a set of schematics. "Virtue Station, which was called something unpronounceable by humans in the original language so I translated."

Gar frowned at the schematics and shrugged. His own path off the planet Luvendan had involved very few stops along the way, and in any case, there were so many planets and stations that no one could hope to know all of them.

"This is the source of the mercenaries Jutkelon summoned?" Gar asked. He was learning to speak English and his speech had gradually grown more formal to match Barnabas', something Shinigami found deeply amusing.

"Not precisely." Barnabas frowned. "All Shinigami could find was that one of those ships had docked at Virtue relatively recently. It could have been nothing more than a stop to refuel or run some unrelated errand. It is likely there is actually nothing here."

"There is *not* nothing," Shinigami countered. "It's an out-of-the-way station frequented by mercenaries, so there's got to be *something* for you to get offended about."

Barnabas looked up at the speakers. "I do not 'get offended,' as you put it. I simply take issue with matters of injustice."

"Yes, you talk very politely while you determine who's pissed you off, then you start ripping spines out. I wouldn't believe it if I hadn't seen it with my own two... Well, sensed it with my... You know what, let's just go with 'seeing' as the verb."

"Indeed." Barnabas returned to his maps.

"How can I help?" Gar asked when he was sure Shinigami and Barnabas were done trading insults. He had already learned not to get in the middle of *those* conversations. There had been one the other day about a game of chess that had resulted in increasingly ridiculous threats he was fairly sure were jokes.

Fairly sure.

He had, however, barely made it out of the way of a thrown chair and several books, and had since made it a personal rule not to be in the same room with them when they played chess. In fact, he would keep at least one airlock-safe door between him and them.

Barnabas stared at the plans with his arms crossed. "I had thought you would come onto the station with me." His brow furrowed in thought as he scanned the schematics. "There is a chance, however slight, that someone will recognize me. If you stay separated from me and are careful about who sees you getting off the ship we'll have an extra pair of eyes." He looked at Gar and his blue eyes bored right into the Luvendi. "Are you up for that?"

Gar wasn't entirely sure what the question meant. Was Barnabas asking whether he felt safe enough to come onto the station, or whether he believed he was ready to be a part of one of Barnabas' operations?

When Gar had helped Barnabas to free the workers in Lan's mine, he had been acting partly out of self-interest. He knew that if he failed to do the right thing Barnabas would kill him. In fact, Gar had believed that Barnabas would let him die when Lan shot him. At the time, he had accepted that as a fitting punishment for his transgressions.

Gar had spent the last few weeks since Barnabas had saved his life thinking about what he wanted to do with his unexpected extension. He had learned the important lesson that some things were worth standing up for no matter the risk, and that he could no longer ignore the voice in his head that told him to do the right thing.

Those sorts of revelations tended to change one's outlook considerably.

He hadn't come to any firm decisions about his next steps, but he *did* know that Barnabas would be going after injustice and doing the right thing. Until Gar figured everything out for himself, he would help Barnabas.

He was not foolish enough to think he'd be given a critical role in any of Barnabas' plans. He still had a lot to prove, after all. But he had to start somewhere.

"I'll go to the station," he told him. "I want to help however I can."

"Good." Barnabas nodded without commenting on any of the turmoil he had sensed in Gar's thoughts and tapped the schematics in front of him. "I'm intending to go *here*. It's a bar—or at least it *should* be one—a few floors above the main level. I should be able to hear something that will lead me to more information. Meanwhile, you'll go here. It's on the main level and there will be less shady stuff going on—"

"Not much less," Shinigami opined. "This place reeks of money laundering. The people in the banks like to dress up, but that doesn't make 'em classy."

"Don't gamble," Barnabas ordered Gar. "And don't look

at anyone oddly. And don't… You know what, *you* go to the first bar. *I'll* stay on the main level."

A raspy chuckle came from the speakers. "Aww, yeah. You're gonna punch some bankers, aren't you?"

"I most certainly am not." Barnabas aimed his rebuke in the direction of one of Shinigami's speakers. "Unless they deserve it," he added under his breath.

"That's what I thought." She sounded smug. "Let me know if you want any backup."

"Missiles on a station? Really?"

"I also have the flamethrower, remember."

"We have not established that."

"No, because you refuse to let me test it."

Barnabas took a deep breath and prayed for patience. "What you're looking for," he told Gar pointedly, "is anyone advertising protection, weaponry, or guard services—that sort of thing. Mention that Jutkelon was a contact and referred you to them. If they're part of whatever group he called on, that will get you in. If not, pretend it was a misunderstanding. Mercenaries generally rely on very unsubtle threats, but they don't like to be known for killing potential clients. As long as you respond appropriately you should be fine."

Gar swallowed. Being a Luvendi, he was remarkably unsuited to combat. His bones were brittle enough that he could not perform manual labor, serve as a guard, or even risk walking along a well-traveled thoroughfare where he would be jostled too often.

It was one of the main reasons the Luvendi were so little-known, and even then only in areas of work such as information brokering or banking. He would suggest working on the main floor, if not for the fact that Barnabas was right—those who did money laundering were not only extremely dangerous in these out-of-the-way stations, they took offense to almost *everything*.

In contrast, those who wanted to sell their services as guards might be physically intimidating, but could usually be mollified by the promise of money. The universe was strange sometimes.

"Don't worry," Shinigami told him. "I've got your back if you need it."

"Thank you," Gar murmured. He didn't say it, but he was fairly sure it would be better not to call on Shinigami unless he was in dire need. He could just imagine the sort of chaos she would find 'helpful.' The bar he was intending to sit in might be rubble by the time she was done.

From Barnabas' expression, he suspected the same thing.

"Do we know *anything* about these people?" Gar asked him.

"Not much, unfortunately. It *is* frustrating." Barnabas sighed. "Jutkelon was clearly part of some larger...syndicate, maybe? Consortium? Or perhaps he simply had favors owed him. Regardless, he was able to call on three armed ships. Their allies, whoever they may be, are likely wondering what happened to them. I could hope of course that those were three totally unrelated captains, all of whom had only one ship and no other connections, but..."

"But?" Gar asked.

Barnabas' mouth took a wry twist. "I've been alive long enough to know that things almost never work out quite so neatly. I'll be looking for anything I can find in the banking part of the station about how these people stored and processed their money, as well as where they got their supplies. Things like munitions might lead us back to a larger group. It might also be a complete mess with too many leads to follow."

Shinigami snickered. "Look at it this way—you get to kill more bad guys."

"That isn't *precisely* my goal."

"Of course it is. You seek out injustice. There's *always* injustice and the people perpetrating it almost never back down, ergo, you have to kill them. This gives you a good place to start, whereas otherwise your choices would amount to an embarrassment of riches. Yeah, that's right— I can talk all flowery, too."

Barnabas looked at the speakers. "Are you done?"

"Not quite. Tabitha told me to tell you that your new hat will make you look like an idiot."

Barnabas' face settled into the pleasant smile Gar had learned to fear more than any frown. "You let her into my rooms?"

"Not so much *let* her as... Well, yes. Yes, I did. You weren't listening to me about how stupid it looked and I wanted her opinion."

There was a dangerous pause, then Barnabas, to Gar's surprise, started laughing.

It was a surprise to Barnabas as well. Part of him took it as a very bad sign that he could find something like this funny. After all, Shinigami had invaded his privacy and then insulted him publicly over a matter of aesthetic taste. He should probably be worried by the fact that he had spent enough time around Tabitha to be amused by that.

On the other hand, the mental image of Tabitha going through his wardrobe and commenting dismissively on things was incredibly funny, and it gave him an idea.

"I don't suppose she tried on the hat?"

Shinigami paused. "She did," the AI replied cautiously after a moment.

"And I don't suppose you have pictures of that?"

Another pause. "I do."

"Oh, this is going to be so good." Barnabas rubbed his hands together. "*So* good. I'm going to need those pictures."

"What are you going to do with them?" Gar couldn't help but be curious.

"Do the Luvendi have anything in the way of holiday greeting cards?"

"No?" Gar looked at the speaker from which he could now hear the AI laughing hysterically. "What's a holiday?"

"You don't have holidays and you don't sing. What do people *do* with their time on Luvendan?"

"Mostly we meditate."

"A whole planet full of monks," Barnabas muttered to Shinigami. "Lord help us."

Shinigami snickered. "And *you* are one to talk?"

"I am the only one on this ship who knows exactly how boring that would be. Well, I suppose Gar does. Never mind. In any case, Gar, in a few months I am going to send a greeting card to Tabitha's acquaintances to wish them a happy and prosperous New Year with a picture of her in that hat."

"She's going to kill you," Shinigami predicted.

"Mmm. She's welcome to try. How long is it until Christmas?"

"More than half a year."

"She'll have forgotten by then," Gar told Barnabas.

"That's what I'm counting on." Barnabas was grinning. "There's a saying on Earth, 'Revenge is a dish best served cold.'"

Gar frowned, trying to interpret the phrase. Since meeting Barnabas he had begun to gather a mental list of phrases that made very little sense to him. There were already quite a few.

"Well, if everyone's clear on the plan, I think we can head out." Barnabas looked up at Shinigami's cameras. "As Bobcat would say, 'Punch it.'"

Another idiom. Gar resisted the urge to groan. He was never going to figure out this language.

"Their engines are warming up!" Tik'ta swiveled her chair to look at her captain.

As usual, she had to work not to laugh. He was pacing the bridge with his hands behind his back. It was an exaggerated gesture meant to emphasize how serious he was, and how impressive it was that he was waiting patiently even though he felt great urgency about...something.

Tik'ta was willing to bet there was no particular matter on his mind. Klafk'tin was a man who clearly aspired to greatness and wanted the Hieto to rise to prominence in the universe, but had yet to demonstrate any hint of achieving his desires.

This job, though... Even Tik'ta had to admit that this job might make the captain's name. He'd found an incredible ship floating around this backwater planet. Its engines were a dream and its weaponry appeared to be top notch, but it didn't seem to have more than a skeleton crew.

In short, it was a perfect target.

"Follow it," Klafk'tin ordered. He puffed up his chest, perhaps reveling in the greatness he would have when it was *his* ship. "What does it say on the prow? What is the ship's name?"

"*Shinigami,* sir. It appears to be a human ship."

"Do you have any idea how valuable it is, then? No one has been able to get their technology." Klafk'tin was practically drooling, though he attempted to look dignified. "I'm going to be rich," he whispered. "The next time it sets down we'll go in and we take it."

3

The bars on the main level of Virtue Station were clean and orderly, with all the hallmarks of catering to the rich: decorative accents, soft music and lighting, expensive materials used in the walls and floors, and real flowers.

And, of course, the obligatory complement of armed guards who were trying not to look like what they were.

Barnabas took a seat near one of them and attempted to look unremarkable and unthreatening by their standards. He had taken care with his outfit. He was wearing a black suit and a crisp white shirt with a blue tie, which Shinigami had pointed out was clearly a vain attempt to bring out his eyes.

He had not deigned to respond to that.

He also wore a pair of slim glasses. Barnabas' vision was perfect, but the glasses had a tiny camera embedded in each temple which would switch between true color, night vision, and infrared as he required. The cameras could swivel to face the side, or look slightly up from his line of sight so he could "look" at something else while carefully examining a target.

He pulled out a tablet and peered at the screen. To anyone else, it would show a standard news page. People often made it a point to catch up on the news when they stopped at stations, and those in the richer districts made use of the official broadcast pages rather than word of mouth.

However, Barnabas did not see the news page at all. Instead, the interaction between the tablet and the glasses gave him a view of what the camera on his earpiece saw. He was able to watch the interior of the nearby bar while he pretended to read.

Above his head, a tiny listening device made to look like an insect darted behind one of the security cameras and went into the bar. Barnabas tapped the edge of the screen to direct it to land near a likely-looking group and settled down to wait.

"Good afternoon, sir." A Torcellan waiter in a well-tailored black tunic and pants laid down a dish of some unidentifiable vegetable and a napkin in anticipation of Barnabas' drink order. "What may I get you?"

"Would you happen to have any fruit juice?" Barnabas asked him.

You have an addiction.

I do not. I merely enjoy the beverage.

"I'll see what we can get you." The waiter looked doubtful. "Do you have any preferences?"

"Hakoj," Barnabas told him. It was the juice Aebura liked to serve. "If you don't have that, surprise me."

After all, it wasn't as if any low-level poison could hurt

him, since his nanocytes would easily take care of it. And to Barnabas' knowledge, no one on this station should know enough about him to want to use a more potent poison.

Yet.

All right. He straightened his back slightly and adjusted the tablet on his crossed legs. *Time to find out if these bankers have anything interesting to say. Let me know if you hear any talk related to anything you found out about those ships.*

Of course. I'm already running their known crew members against a list of the patrons at these bars.

What about the banks?

The bars are *the banks. You do your business while you get a drink. Come to think of it, we should make that the standard in the Federation. Deposit your money, get a drink. It's an experience, not a transaction.*

Sometimes your business acumen worries me. Just keep me updated, and we'll see who comes to find us.

Gar made his way through Virtue Station slowly. Barnabas had told him to take his time, so he was. He paused at some of the vendors' stalls and inspected their wares. Certain fruits and vegetables were available, types that stored easily for long distance travel in space. Most of them weren't anyone's favorite, but it was remarkable just how much the palate craved fresh food after living on preserved meals and nutritional paste.

The main level hadn't had any of this. It was entirely given over to the "legitimate" and high-grossing business interests of the station—namely, banking. Gar had only seen a glimpse of it before he was shuffled off onto the other levels. The guards on the main level were careful to let through only those who looked as though they had the funds and temperament for monetary activities.

Once one got away from the main floor the station quickly came to resemble any other station Gar had ever been on. It had been built as a series of corridors, each lined with shops and apartments. Commerce, however, had spilled into the corridors, so that there was only a narrow path to walk in between the blankets and carts that lined the thoroughfares.

Gar walked carefully, trying not to bump into anyone. He knew that the Pod-doc on the *Shinigami* could repair any fractured bones, but he had spent a lifetime without any such resources and it would take time to unlearn his innate caution.

It was reflex to turn his body so he wouldn't collide with other pedestrians. It was habit to walk through the least-traveled areas of the corridor.

At least the people here seemed to be accustomed to Luvendi. Many even went out of their way to avoid bumping into him, which Gar made sure to thank them for. One never knew when a kind word or a single gesture might come back in the form of desperately-needed help. He had watched Lan go through life treating the polite actions of others as no more than his due. Lan had ended up with almost no allies, and certainly no one who would speak up for him.

Gar was determined not to end up the same way, but he did wonder if this was only self-interest speaking again. At heart, he still wasn't sure if he had the makings of a fitting ally for Barnabas—and he was afraid of what would happen if Barnabas decided he did not.

He put those thoughts aside and made his way up to the floor Barnabas had specified. As Barnabas had told him, there was a bar here. Gar approached the dingy entrance, where the two hulking Brakalon guards proceeded to shout at Gar to stand still for a weapons scan.

He complied and they let him through, but only after looking him up and down suspiciously, as if to ask what he wanted in a place like this.

The same thing everyone else here wants, Gar thought acidly. He was clearly not a person who could fight on his own, and the bar was full of people who could. It made a great deal of sense that he was here.

He went to the bar to buy a drink first. This allowed him to see the layout of the bar and get a feel for the conversation around him, and it made sure that he wouldn't get the evil eye from the bartender. Businesses didn't like it when you loitered.

Even before Gar's drink arrived he knew his target. There were plenty of shadowed alcoves in this bar, and two Shrillexians had walked by him on their way to one, growling to one another about what kind of ship could take on three.

As Barnabas would say, "Bingo!"

Gar still needed to figure out the origin of the phrase, since every time he searched the results were a strange game with number-filled squares. Clearly, his dictionary was broken. He'd have to talk to Shinigami about that.

In the meantime, he looped around the bar and took a

circuitous route toward the alcove where the two Shrillex-ians were now sitting. Unfortunately, the acoustics of the bar had been well-designed so that people inside the alcoves could speak with relative privacy.

Cursing, Gar eased himself forward, trying to catch even a snippet of conversation—

"What do you want, spy?" The words came from behind him, and they came with the distinctive sound of a Shrillexian voice.

His blood seemed to turn to ice. Gar turned and looked at the Shrillexian, then made a show of looking in the alcove. He knew what had happened, though. He thought he'd been stealthy but all the while they'd known he was there and they'd circled around behind him.

He was terrible at this.

There was only one thing for it, and that was to act well enough that they didn't shoot him right here. "Are you…" He made a show of trying to pronounce a name but finally settled for, "The Shrillexian I've been hearing about? The mercenary. They say you *always* complete your jobs?"

It was a gamble, and a dangerous bluff, but Gar had chosen his lie well. The Shrillexian gave a dangerous smile and puffed his chest out a bit.

"I am Fedden, yes."

"Fedden!" Gar said the name as if he'd been reminded of it. "Yes. Look, I really need your help. A contact suggested you to me. I wasn't sure you'd talk to me, but if you're free to take a job…"

His heart was pounding. If Fedden took offense to anything he said, Gar could be well and truly dead by the time Barnabas got there to help. Even the Shinigami's medical Pods wouldn't be able to help with that.

But Fedden gave a sharp-toothed smile and gestured to the booth. "Tell me about your problem and I'll tell you if I'm available."

Well, this is interesting, Shinigami commented.

Barnabas jumped. His video feed of the two bankers had been interrupted by a view from Gar's perspective as he spoke to two Shrillexians.

Shinigami, what am I looking at?

While Gar was under, I decided to install a chip in what I was fairly sure was his audio-visual processing center. He took to it remarkably well.

You mean that he did not immediately drop dead.

Yes, that.

And now we're spying on him.

Right again.

That was unethical.

Shinigami said nothing, but Barnabas had the impression that she would be rolling her eyes if she were human. At his elbow, the waiter appeared once more with an apologetic expression.

"I'm very sorry, sir. It appears we have no hakoj juice. However, the bartender sent along this cocktail with his compliments."

"Thank you very much," Barnabas told him. He made a show of tipping the man an extravagant amount, knowing that several people would notice the money and want to speak to him soon.

When the waiter had gone, after a very deep bow and profuse thanks, Barnabas took a sip of the drink. *Shinigami, can you analyze this for me, please?*

Some preserved fruit juices, sweeteners, and of course, alcohol. It looks like the suspension facilitates a very slow release into your bloodstream.

So you get drunk without noticing it?

Pretty much. What's it like to get drunk?

Well, it inhibits cognitive processing, so if you're curious, I could just whack one of your servers with a mallet and we can see what that does. Or perhaps just switch a bunch of connections around at random.

Shinigami radiated silent horror.

Believe it or not, Barnabas told her, *it's quite fun.*

Are you sure? It doesn't sound *like fun.*

Perhaps it's an acquired taste. Barnabas took another sip and sensed the nanocytes swinging into action. He certainly wasn't going to get drunk, not with the settings he'd given himself. His body neutralized all poisons, alcohol included. *Back to Gar. I would rather not spy on his thoughts unless it's necessary.*

First, you always think it's necessary. Second, this isn't about his thoughts, it's about his actions. Your whole purpose in bringing him was to determine whether he is a potential ally or a self-centered douche-canoe.

Tabitha again?

She also suggested "cock-monkey," just as a general term—not specifically about Gar. I've been waiting for the right moment to use it.

Keep me posted. Barnabas settled back in his seat. *And you've made your point. Let's see what Gar does when he doesn't know we're watching.*

Right. Also, heads up—there's a munitions dealer in the bank who might be connected to the mercenary ships. I'm trying to get into his accounts now.

Excellent. Barnabas gave a satisfied smile and settled down to watch Gar's performance.

Gar leaned on the sticky table and tried desperately to think of what he might say next. There was one gambit that might work well, of course, but it was so directly applicable to the Shrillexians' problems that they might get suspicious.

So he embroidered the truth somewhat selectively.

"Did you hear about what happened on Devon recently?

They exchanged a look. He definitely had their attention, but Fedden made a show of leaning back in his seat. "Why don't you tell us," the mercenary challenged.

So he was at least a little bit clever. Gar shrugged. "The company that owned the mines got bought out and they all got closed down...unless we wanted to reopen them and give the workers what *they* thought were good contracts." He made a show of snorting, as if to say this was plainly ridiculous. "I tried that, but I think you can guess how it went. Now I'm looking to relocate."

This put them off-balance, as he'd meant it to. He had essentially told them he knew all about Devon but hadn't been directly involved in anything that had happened there recently.

"What're you coming to *us* for?" Fedden asked.

"Jutkelon recommended you," Gar bluffed. This was the dangerous part, but it seemed a worthwhile risk. "I went to him a couple of weeks ago and asked him if he'd staff a mine off-planet. He wanted to stay local, but he said maybe you'd know someone."

Fedden and the other Shrillexian looked at one another for a moment and Gar held his breath.

Then Fedden smiled and leaned forward again. "Let's talk specifics, then. I think you and I can deal. And I think maybe you'll be able to help us with something else, too."

In the docking bay, Klafk'tin strolled down the gangway of the *Gruwa* and looked around. Virtue Station was fairly well-staffed, but there still weren't enough dockworkers to linger outside ships that had clearly already been unloaded and vetted.

Which meant the *Shinigami*—which had been here for a couple of hours now—did not merit even a single glance from the people hurrying by.

Excellent.

Klafk'tin pointed a scanner casually at the ship and gave a chuckle when it came back saying that there were no life forms aboard.

"Get ready," he told his crew. "We need to do this quick. Let's take that ship and get out of here before anyone's the wiser."

4

_____

I *think this is going well,* Barnabas remarked offhand to Shinigami. In his opinion, Gar was showing a good sense of subtlety in his dealings with Fedden.

The only problem was that Fedden clearly knew something about High Tortuga, and Barnabas wished he were there to scan the Shrillexian's mind. If he'd gone there and had Gar come here, they'd know exactly what it was that Fedden wanted help with.

Because it looked like someone was searching for them, too.

But *who?*

Barnabas was just about to mention this to Shinigami when a Brakalon sat down opposite him. There was no request as to whether the seat was taken, nor did he ask if Barnabas was busy. It was clear that there would be a discussion between the two, and it would happen now.

Barnabas smiled pleasantly at him. "Good afternoon."

The Brakalon did not acknowledge the greeting, just sat back in his chair, his posture nominally relaxed. However, it only served to show the outline of the weapon under his jacket, and he was clearly ready to move quickly if it came to a fight.

Barnabas did not move at all. The Brakalon was not making a scene, and Barnabas saw no need to make one either.

Yet.

"There's a listening device in the bar," the Brakalon commented. His gaze was on the people in the pretty park area of the main floor as he spoke. "Mr. Jodu wants to know if it might be yours."

"It is," Barnabas agreed simply.

The Brakalon turned his attention to him and narrowed his eyes.

"I'm new to Virtue Station," Barnabas explained. "I hear any number of useful activities take place near this very bar. I need to ascertain which people here would be the correct ones to approach—and which would not."

Shinigami snickered. *I like it when you're sneaky.*

None of what I said was a lie.

You meant to make him think you're a banker who needs illicit business done, and he probably does think that. You misled him.

I create opportunities, Barnabas clarified with great dignity. *Ones that allow moral people to show their fortitude and immoral people to show their lack of it.*

Mmmhmm. You know, you have your head so far up your—

There was a pause.

Shinigami?

Another pause. *How busy would you say you are?*

Well, he just put his hand on his gun, so I'm not exactly unengaged.

Ah. Never mind then.

What's going on?

A minor matter, nothing to worry about. You talk to him. I'll brief you when you get back to the ship.

Barnabas frowned mentally, but his face held a pleasant smile when he looked at the Brakalon. "Clearly, your employer is offended by my use of listening devices. Perhaps he would be prepared to provide me with accurate information regarding the trustworthiness and provenance of those inside the bar. In specific, I've had difficulty finding someone to provide quality munitions on a reliable schedule." He folded his hands in his lap. "And I want to be very clear that I will take *great* offense if I later learn I have been given inaccurate information."

The Brakalon froze. He had been here to threaten Barnabas. He might not run the show, but he knew—just like many large beings who beat compliance into people for a living—that when someone smaller than him did not seem afraid, there just *might* be a reason for it.

"I'll speak to Mr. Jodu," he demurred and disappeared.

Shinigami? Shinigami?

Kind of busy here. Look, I'll, uh... I think you have an open line to get to some of those people at the bar. You really should follow up on that while you have the chance. Mustafee Boreir is the Yofu at the bar—blue skin, eyes on the side of his head? That one. He owns a munitions group that might have supplied Galagg and Jutkelon.

Excellent, thank you. Now, if you—

Gotta go!

Strange. Barnabas stood up, buttoned his suit jacket, and strolled to the bar to meet his first set of targets.

Gar's communications unit buzzed at his wrist. **When you are free, come to the docking bay but do not come within sight of the ship. -S**

He frowned at the message. What was Shinigami up to?

The only thing he knew was that she had reasons for everything she did. Perhaps there was about to be a scene on the station and they needed to get out quickly. 'When you are free' suggested the matter wasn't extremely urgent, however.

Gar looked up at the two Shrillexians with a smile. They had made some good progress, and he laid a card with his contact details on the table.

"There is a matter that requires my attention, I'm afraid. Funding for the mining equipment. Underwriting. I'm sure you understand." He waved a hand to indicate everyone's universal annoyance with the paperwork required to start a business. "Most importantly...contact me about the matter you said I might help with. If we are to do business together, a benefit to one of us is a benefit to both."

It was a flowery sentiment that he did not entirely believe, but he was interested to see how Fedden and his second-in-command would describe their problem with Barnabas.

Because Gar was very sure *that* was the matter they wanted help with.

He made his way as quickly as possible to the main level, avoiding the temptation to detour down back hallways. If there was trouble, he should make it as difficult as possible for anything unfortunate to happen to him.

He was back at the docks soon, showing his ID to a very disinterested security guard. Apparently there wasn't a fight yet, then. What was all this about?

He tapped his communications unit. "Shinigami, can we—"

It buzzed: **Text only.**

Gar sighed and began typing: **What's wrong?**

There are several people who I believe are trying to steal the ship. They're setting up some equipment near me and they have someone keeping watch for guards.

Gar felt a stab of alarm. **Why haven't you called Barnabas in?**

He's getting some information right now. I didn't want to disturb him.

I really think he'd want you to tell him about this!

Fine, it's a bet. In the meantime, I'd appreciate it if you'd scare them off. I don't want to let them know I'm on board.

Gar gave a sigh. She seemed to have forgotten the particulars of their situation.

Are you still there? Shinigami asked. **Now would be best for an intervention.**

I'm a Luvendi, Gar typed back, annoyed. **I'm not going to intimidate anyone, and I can't let this turn into a fight. They aren't mercenaries, so I can't hire them. What do you want me to do?**

Think of something! Steal a security uniform.

Again, there is one of me, and I'm Luvendi. Luvendi never work security.

This is a nightmare. Why haven't you people turned into brains in jars at this point if your bodies are so useless?

That is incredibly insulting. Just because I can't fight doesn't make me useless. Silence was his only answer, and Gar sighed. **Fine. I'll think of something. But for the record, I think we'd still be better off getting Barnabas back.**

He sank down onto a bench and racked his brain. How the hell did you convince a bunch of people who were already stealing a ship that a lone Luvendi was dangerous enough to fear?

He was so engaged in his thoughts that he didn't notice the security cameras of the nearby *Gruwa* trained right on him.

In the alcove of the bar two stories up Fedden drained his glass and smiled. Even the burn of the terrible liquor did nothing to dull his mood.

Things had been unsettled lately in the syndicate. Their leader Crallus had always been useless in Fedden's opinion, but lately he'd started getting on their cases more, too. He wanted to know every detail of every job, and he never said why when he was asked.

When Jutkelon sent a message from Devon, Crallus had made it a point to send three ships. It was a big show

—"Fucking overkill," Fedden had said several times to his second-in-command—and Crallus had gone on and on and fucking *on* about how he was sending his three *best* ships.

Well, the joke was on him, because all three ships had been blown out of orbit without so much as a chance to send a distress signal, and now Crallus was scrambling to get information. He'd promised a bounty to any ship that dropped what they were doing and found out more about the ship from Devon. It was a human ship named *Shinigami*. Apparently no one knew who flew it.

But Fedden might just have an in to get those details now. That Luvendi had no idea how valuable his knowledge might be, but if he'd spoken to Jutkelon in the last few weeks, he might very well know the name of the human who'd been a thorn in Jutkelon's side.

Fedden was going to bring the Luvendi in, get his information, and make Crallus show how much he wanted it in cold hard cash.

"Send a message to this channel," he instructed Tagurn. He passed over the card with the source address. It didn't give much away about who the person might be, which Fedden supposed made sense for a slaver from Devon. "Tell him to meet us at the base and we'll talk details. We'll make Crallus pay for the information, then we'll go take a contract with this guy. If he wants to set up mines, he'll need a lot of guards." He smiled, showing a lot of teeth. "Our luck is turning around."

"Captain?" Tik'ta's voice came over Klafk'tin's earpiece. "We may have a problem."

"Yes? What is it?" Klafk'tin's voice was jovial. He was in a fairly good mood and decided not to let any impending problems sour it.

"One of the crew members of the *Shinigami* is back in the docking bay."

"What?" Klafk'tin looked around and cursed. He should have known at least one of them would come back before too long. It had been stupid to leave the ship unattended so far. "Where are they?"

"He's just sitting on a bench near the checkpoint."

Klafk'tin relaxed fractionally and gave an annoyed sigh. "Then why are you bothering me?"

"Because I don't know what he's up to." Tik'ta's voice was clipped now. "If he gets closer, he's only a couple of moments' walk from being able to see you. I thought it might be relevant to your planning."

Klafk'tin threw an annoyed glance in the direction of the *Gruwa*. Tik'ta was a very competent pilot, but she had never been very polite. She didn't do anything he could specifically point to as rude, but during moments like these he could sense she didn't think much of his leadership.

He resolved to speak to her about that—right after he stole this ship. After all, she'd probably be more compliant if faced with the choice between continuing to fly the *Gruwa* and getting to pilot the *Shinigami* instead. He'd seen her salivating over those engines.

"On the double," he snapped to his crew. "We may have company soon. Get the doors open *now*."

Wohva gave him an annoyed look but didn't say

anything. She was a very good electrical engineer, and Klafk'tin knew she was worth far more than he paid her. The thing was, without any experience, she couldn't prove that to the captains of any bigger ships. He should probably raise her salary if they got this ship.

When they got this ship.

It was as good as theirs now. One solitary crew member was hardly going to stand between them and taking it. A bullet, a bribe to the security guard…

Yes, it would be easy enough to accomplish.

"Captain, the doors should be open in a moment." Wohva put her tools down and turned them off carefully.

Klafk'tin gave an impatient sigh. Now was not the time for safety protocols.

Wohva ignored him. She typed a command into the tiny box she had linked up with the doors and smiled in satisfaction when they slid open. She nodded to Klafk'tin.

"The ship is yours."

Gar sat up suddenly. **I have an idea**, he typed. **It's risky, but right now it's all I can think of if you are certain we shouldn't expose your presence**.

He explained, and Shinigami barely hesitated.

I like it. Get ready.

"Captain." Wohva and the rest stood back.

Klafk'tin took a moment to admire the hull. A perfect

ship, just begging for someone to steal it. With it docked at a station and totally unattended, its weapons were useless. Now he just needed to do one last thing.

"Harrdrack." He nodded to the surly Shrillexian. "Make sure they don't have any booby-traps in place."

He didn't like Harrdrack much. Like every Shrillexian Klafk'tin had ever met Harrdrack enjoyed fighting, so he had signed on at a reasonable price, but he wasn't careful and he was prone to disobeying orders.

Now he barely even grunted when he headed up the gangway. He passed Wohva and Klafk'tin and stepped into the interior of the ship.

Or he would have if the doors hadn't slammed shut with a crunch of bones and a spurt of blood.

Wohva screamed and clapped a hand over her mouth and Klafk'tin looked away in distaste. He had warned Harrdrack that there might be booby-traps, and the male still hadn't been careful. Had there been a tripwire hidden beneath the doors, perhaps? Or maybe—

"Captain!" It was Tik'ta's voice.

But she was too late. "Hello," a smooth voice said from some distance away. Klafk'tin turned, and his jaw dropped open.

A Luvendi? Really?

Gar was praying to every deity he'd ever heard of, including the strange amorphous one Barnabas had mentioned a few times. Underneath the robes, his body was drenched in sweat and both of his hearts were beating erratically and so fast he thought they might burst.

"I see you're trying to steal my ship." He tried to speak the way Barnabas did; as if he weren't afraid of anything. "As you can see, you've made a mistake. Nevertheless, given that you've paid for it—" he looked at the doors and forced himself not to look too nauseated as he gestured to his communications unit, pretending he had orchestrated the doors snapping shut, "I will give you one chance to walk away."

For a moment, he had them. They wavered and looked at one another nervously. Gar sighed and pretended to wait patiently. *Please let them walk away, please let them walk away...*

Then their leader pulled a gun. "I have twenty more crew members." He grinned nastily. "You probably don't have that many booby-traps. I'll get your ship with or without you."

The crew gave him an incredulous look and Gar's stomach seemed to drop out of his torso. If they couldn't get in, they couldn't get him to the medical Pods. If he got shot now he was going to die.

Barnabas stepped out of the shadows at the other end of the hangar, "You know, that really isn't the best way to boost your crew's morale."

5

Barnabas' eyes swept the scene. Gar stood strong. Barnabas had to hand it to him; the Luvendi was bluffing very well. He seemed for all the world to be unafraid of the gun pointed at him. If Barnabas hadn't known better he might have believed that Gar had booby-trapped the *Shinigami* himself.

But Barnabas *did* know better, because he knew Shinigami. Smashing someone between the doors when they had let their guard down had her rather distinctive flair.

He was also pleased to note that his choice to come directly back to the shuttle bay rather than speak to Mustafee Boreir had been the correct one. With a name and a window into their data streams, Shinigami could get good information with or without Barnabas talking to the Yofu.

That was, if she didn't get stolen—as these people were clearly trying to do.

"Who are you?" an alien asked. He was a species Barnabas didn't recognize, very broad-shouldered but not tall. There was a faint greenish cast to his skin if one looked closely.

"I am Barnabas."

"That name means nothing to me." The alien sneered.

"It doesn't have to," Barnabas told him. "It's not the important part of what's about to happen."

"Which is?" The alien looked at his crew with a contemptuous smile.

None of them smiled back. They'd all heard him say they were expendable and they clearly weren't very happy with him right now.

"You should start with an apology to your crew," Barnabas stated gravely. He linked his hands behind his back and strolled closer.

"For what?"

Barnabas said a silent prayer for patience. This alien really was remarkably dim-witted.

"For saying that you would use them to check for booby-traps," he explained patiently. "Surely that is not in their job description. It is also a horrendous way to treat one's crew."

"It's their job if I *say* it's their job." The alien scoffed. "I am Klafk'tin, captain of the *Gruwa*, and my crew does what I tell them to do!"

"I see." Barnabas glanced at the sullen faces of the crew. None of them looked happy about his words, but none of them were mutinying either. That was disappointing. "We're still going to start with an apology."

"Why?"

"Because I said so." Barnabas allowed a hint of command to enter his voice.

"Listen," Klafk'tin told him, "you humans might think you're real special, with your Empress and your technology, but you aren't any better than anyone else."

"She's not the Empress anymore, but I quite agree," Barnabas responded equably. "The measure of a person is in their actions, not in their species. Why, some of the most distinguished members of the former Etheric Empire were Yollin."

Klafk'tin glared at him. "Don't change the subject."

"I wouldn't dream of it. What did *you* think we were talking about?"

"About you backing off and giving me the ship that I rightfully took off your hands!"

"'Rightfully?'" Barnabas frowned. "That doesn't sound correct. And you still haven't apologized."

"I'm not going to! I'm not some Yollin you can just order around!"

"You mean that you're not someone like your crew, who you feel perfectly justified in ordering around." Barnabas shook his head. "You have no idea of the concept of power, do you? To you, it simply means that others must do as you say and you do not need to give them anything in return. Would that be correct?"

"Yes." Klafk'tin glared, then saw the expressions on his crew's faces. "I give 'em wages," he told Barnabas. "There's lodging."

"Wages and a place to sleep *inside* the ship sounds like the bare minimum expected of an employer," Barnabas observed. "You've miscalculated, Klafk'tin."

"Oh? And how's that?"

"I am not a member of your crew." Barnabas allowed his voice to deepen as he strode forward. "I do not take orders from you." He unbuttoned his suit jacket and shrugged out of it, throwing it neatly over a nearby crate. There was no reason to treat such a fine suit disrespectfully, after all. With his Jean Dukes Specials holstered but now visible, he continued toward Klafk'tin with a dangerous smile. "And you just tried to steal my ship."

Klafk'tin swiveled to point his gun at Barnabas. "As soon as you're dead, I *did* steal your ship."

Barnabas moved in a blur and there was a crack, a scream, and a clatter as Klafk'tin's gun fell uselessly to the ground. Barnabas kicked it away as the alien stumbled back clutching his lower arm, which seemed to be useless below the elbow.

Barnabas smiled coldly. "Whatever you are, apparently your elbows lock. Convenient." He adjusted his cuffs. "This is your last chance, Klafk'tin. Apologize to your crew and step aside so that another and more deserving member of the crew may take your place as captain."

"Someone shoot him!" Klafk'tin stumbled backward. His face was a shade that, whatever his species, was clearly not healthy. "One of you!"

"They're not helping you," Barnabas observed. "Why do you think that is?"

Klafk'tin bared his teeth at Barnabas in a snarl.

HA! Shinigami didn't try to hide her amusement. *You should really snarl back, your teeth are much more impressive.*

I prefer to reserve that for special moments. By the way, we're going to have a talk about what you think is important enough to tell me about.

Noted.

Barnabas stared at Klafk'tin. "No answer? Very well, then. Klafk'tin, you are relieved of your command of the *Gruwa*. You who were once part of his crew may do as you like. Pick a new captain if you want, but stop taking things that are not yours. Is that clear?"

They nodded, wide-eyed and silent. None of them seemed to know what to say.

"*Fine!*" Klafk'tin snarled. He stumbled a few steps and grabbed his gun with his working hand. "If none of you will shoot this bastard, I will!"

"I wouldn't," Barnabas warned.

Klafk'tin gritted his teeth in concentration and swung his good arm with the pistol shaking at the end of it.

They never saw Barnabas' hands move, but there was the distinctive *crack-boom* of a Jean Dukes Special and Klafk'tin's body was thrown across the shuttle bay into a pile of crates.

Barnabas looked at the body. He looked at the gun. He looked back at the body.

What ammo was I using?

Oh, did I forget to mention? There's a note from Jean for you in the armory.

You were just waiting to see how long it took me to notice, weren't you?

I thought it would be a fun surprise. It's impressive, isn't it?

Barnabas holstered the weapon and looked around himself. "Are there any questions?"

They shook their heads.

NATALIE GREY & MICHAEL ANDERLE

"Who do *you* think should be put in charge?" he asked.

Everyone looked back to the *Gruwa*, where an alien was standing on the gangway. From her coloring and build Barnabas guessed she was the same species as Klafk'tin.

To her credit, she had the courage to walk across the bay to the *Shinigami*. She looked down at Klafk'tin's body, but apart from a faint tightening of her lips she did not react to his death.

"The crew seems to think you will be in charge after this," Barnabas told her.

"I probably will." She swallowed. "I am Tik'ta. Is there any further business you have with us?"

"I assume you heard my instruction to stop stealing ships."

She nodded. "I did."

"Would you care to explain why you were here, working with such a captain?"

"Employment is employment, and there's not enough of it to go around." She did not sugarcoat her words. "We draw the line at murder—you saw that no one shot at you even when Klafk'tin ordered it—but stealing?" She shrugged. "Still, if you say not to do it again, we won't. I don't want to get on your bad side."

"I'll take it," Barnabas remarked drily. "Now go. And spread the word, if ever it comes up, that the *Shinigami* is well-defended."

Tik'ta's lips quirked and for a moment he thought she might argue, but instead she nodded and jerked her head at the crew, who followed her back across the docking bay to the *Gruwa*. They stopped to pick up Klafk'tin's body. Barnabas noticed that no one seemed to do any particular grieving over it.

He shook his head and headed up the stairs to the doors.

I don't suppose you have some way to clean these.

Not really, no.

I'll call a deck crew, then...and tip them very heavily.

Gar had come to stand next to Barnabas and he stared at the remains of the Shrillexian. "Klafk'tin clearly knew the ship might be booby-trapped," he commented finally. "He sent the Shrillexian in first on purpose."

"Yes." Barnabas headed back down the gangway to get his jacket. "The universe hasn't lost very much now that he's dead, I think. Good thinking on your feet back there. If their captain hadn't been so devoted to taking anything he could and killing anyone who stood in his way you might have won that one."

Gar's look was more than a little bit frustrated. "It's all a game to you, isn't it?"

"I beg your pardon?" Barnabas' eyebrows went up in surprise.

"You said you thought I might have won that one. Did it occur to you that if I had lost I would be dead? I'm not as resilient as you are. You can take bullets and keep walking, and you heal almost instantly. You and Shinigami talk about coming up with plans as if no matter what happens we'll all survive, but I might not. Shinigami, open the doors, please." Gar lifted his robes up and stepped over the mess on the coaming without looking at it and disappeared without waiting for a reply.

He has a point, you know.

Barnabas made a face. *Do you think he should be upgraded? Now, when we still do not entirely understand his motivations?*

If you ask me, I don't think even he understands his motivations. And no. But he's correct that we shouldn't be making plans as if he were another Ranger.

Barnabas sighed. *Have you called the deck crew?*

Yes. Don't change the subject.

What do you think we should do, then? Barnabas put his suit jacket back on and leaned against one of the crates.

I told you. Start planning as if we only have the two of us for combat.

The one of us for combat.

How many times do I have to mention the flamethrower?

Barnabas pushed himself up and paced around the deck, considering.

Shinigami was correct, and so was Gar. Gar could have died on this mission. In fact, he nearly *had* died twice. Despite that he had yet to back down, and he hadn't tried to weasel his way out of anything. In fact…

A thought occurred to Barnabas and he narrowed his eyes.

Shinigami, did Gar tell you at any point that he refused to help you against those people?

No. He told me it was a risk to him, but he accepted it when I said it was important.

Barnabas nodded. Gar had not gone running to Barnabas, nor had he turned tail and fled. He hadn't tried to make a deal with anyone unsavory, either.

Despite himself, Barnabas smiled. Gar was already miles different from the man he had been when Barnabas first met him, and so far the changes were good. Barnabas was intrigued to see what would happen in the future.

However, he first had to deal with a deck crew that was going to be deeply upset and then a station manager who wasn't likely to be any happier. It would be hours before he could get back to the bar. Maybe he should ask Gar to handle this part?

Shinigami, is Mustafee Boreir still at the bar?

No, he left not long after you spoke to the guard. The owner of the bar came out to speak to him and he went straight to his ship. They seem to have known you were a threat, but I have no idea how.

Barnabas' eyes narrowed. Why would the guard immediately assume Barnabas was someone a munitions dealer should run away from rather than treating him as a prospective client?

This definitely required more information.

With a sigh, he buttoned his suit jacket, put on his most winning smile, and waited for the bureaucrats to arrive.

6

Gar appeared in the doorway of the main lounge area a while later. When he saw the chessboard and the holographic projection of Baba Yaga he started to back out of the room at once.

"I'll come back."

"It's quite all right," Barnabas assured him. "We haven't started playing yet."

"Which means Barnabas hasn't pissed me off just yet." The holographic projection smiled. By now, Shinigami had begun moving her lips when she spoke.

Unfortunately, she had also started sometimes making her voice come out of every speaker, not just the one on the chair, which had the effect of making the whole thing incredibly unsettling. Shinigami liked to say it was like being a god, mostly because it made Barnabas wince.

Barnabas gave her a look now. "It means Shinigami hasn't pissed *me* off," he corrected and tilted his head at Gar. "What did you want to discuss?"

"I heard from Fedden." Gar hovered in the doorway,

clearly ready to flee at the first sign of trouble. "He gave me the coordinates for a moon called Zahal. It's in the Adhira system, the first moon around the second planet out. The only problem is..."

"He doesn't yet know you will arrive on the ship that took out his colleagues?" Barnabas guessed.

"Yes, that."

"And you're wondering how we're going to dock without him figuring it out?"

"Also that."

"I'll consider some strategies. You do the same." Barnabas began to roll up his sleeves. "For now, you should probably leave if you don't want to be part of the fight." Gar left with a swish and a flick of his robes, and Barnabas smiled across the board at Shinigami. "First move?"

"I'd insist on a coin toss if I hadn't found that coin you made that has two heads." She slid a piece out.

"I wouldn't have had to make it if you hadn't clearly rigged the coin flip algorithm you were using." Barnabas gave her a long look and considered the board.

"Make a move, already. I swear you do this to drive me mad."

"Is it working? Are your servers melting?"

"I'm far more resilient than that."

"I'll just need to try harder, then. Would you like some tea?" He stood up and went over to the little half-kitchen beside the couch. "And don't even think of tampering with the board while I'm gone."

He looked over in time to see it fuzz as several pieces moved hastily back into place, after which Shinigami sat in sullen silence until he returned. Barnabas set a cup at her elbow.

"What is this for?"

"You wish to behave more like a human, and this will enhance the illusion. Also, it's polite—although it's actually just a cup of hot water. One has to draw the line somewhere."

"You were already being insane." Shinigami narrowed her eyes at a piece on the board which suddenly moved of its own accord. "Are you doing that with your mind? What, are you trying to convince someone who comes in here that *you're* the holograph and I'm the real one?"

"Think of the havoc we could wreak," Barnabas suggested. He took a sip of tea and smiled at Shinigami over the rim.

She tilted her head to the side, intrigued. "When would someone be on the ship?"

"Well, someone tried to steal it recently. We could start there. Perhaps at some point, someone sneaks onto the ship, sees me lit like a projection, gets scared by someone they think is real—you'd be wearing armor in this scenario —and... What are you smiling at?"

"Most of your plans center around deception. It's an interesting character aspect in someone who is otherwise so morally ironclad."

"It is not... Oh, very well. Ploys. Tricks."

"Which are?"

"Morally equivalent to lying." Barnabas took another sip of tea somewhat grumpily. "Are you going to move?"

"I'm considering. Also, I wanted to see how long it would take you to ask about it." She switched to mental speech. *Have you given any more thought to what we should do with Gar?*

Some. He watched as she finally made her move and went through the now-familiar habit of checking the board from multiple angles to make sure she'd moved the piece he thought she had. Both of them had tried variants on that trick recently and now Barnabas wore a special pair of glasses while playing.

He never left them unattended.

You aren't suggesting anything, she pressed. *Does that mean you're at a loss?*

He nodded and sighed, then took another sip of tea. *This is very good. Where did we get it?*

Carter was able to acquire some of it. It's an herb the Ubuara use for seasoning. It has mild hallucinogenic properties, by the way. Are you seeing anything strange?

Well, you don't seem to be cheating yet. Does that count?

She flashed him a smile. *I didn't bother to mention it because I assumed your nanocytes would take care of the more unusual aspects of the herb.*

They are. You should probably warn Gar, though. Although... I wonder if that's why he spent all of last evening staring at his hands?

From Shinigami's sudden silence, Barnabas had the sneaking suspicion he was correct. His mouth twitched slightly. Gar had been such a quiet shipmate that Barnabas had assumed what he was seeing was some form of meditation.

Apparently, he had been wrong.

You should probably mention it to him before he does it again.

It would be more fun if—

Shinigami.

Fine. You with your ethics and your moral equivalence and your... I'll come up with a third thing, just give me a moment. She frowned at Barnabas' move. *That's what you're going with? Really?*

Barnabas frowned back. *Since trash talk is a time-honored part of competition I won't outright ban you from using it, but I really do find it a waste.*

She made her move without any further comment on that score. *So, the way I see it, we have a bit of a problem. If we want to get more information out of Fedden without him catching on to who Gar is working for, we need to send Gar in alone. We should also find some way to mask my identity so that they don't figure it all out.*

I could just fight my way past Fedden's crew and take the information out of his head. That would tip our hand somewhat, though, don't you think?

Yes, but Gar had a good point that he's rather...breakable. Barnabas made a move and wondered if Shinigami had figured it out yet. Her self-imposed limit of looking at probabilities only ten turns ahead meant that he had begun building strategies that hinged on twenty or thirty moves. It was an interesting exercise, and one that required a lot of improvisation.

He enjoyed it a surprising amount.

In fact, he enjoyed the entire process of the game they played around their game. Both he and Shinigami understood implicitly that in this battle of wits there was only one real goal: surprise the other person. Barnabas had opened by playing a game he didn't intend to win and had continued with board modifications. Shinigami had retaliated rather spectacularly by making the board zap him every time he touched it, as well as by splitting the holographs so that each piece appeared in multiple places.

Each used conversation to distract the other. Barnabas had succeeded more than once in capturing Shinigami's attention with an interesting dilemma and then making his move while she was calculating probabilities and researching relevant background information. She, of course, had done much the same thing.

Both Barnabas and Shinigami understood the same thing about strategy: there was no playing fair, and there were no givens. One's opponent might have very different goals than expected, and might at any time decide to change the rules of engagement.

Barnabas had an internal bet going with himself, wondering how long it would take before their games involved actual missiles.

Poor Gar.

Barnabas came to a decision after another minute. *We'll do a combination of operations. We'll send Gar in and mask the ship—well, if he's okay with that. At the same time, you will shut down outbound communications without them knowing about it. If things go south, I can clean up the place and we can go for their allies before anyone knows they're dead.*

I like that. Shinigami nodded as she made her move. *You can't make that move,* she added, when Barnabas moved his piece. *There's a piece there.*

There is not— Oh, son of a bitch. Did you change the color of your pieces? Also, they're tiny now.

Shinigami grinned. *I look forward to your retaliation. I hope it will befit a worthy opponent.*

Barnabas narrowed his eyes at her. It *would* be a fitting retaliation. He just had to think of something first—something other than dumping his tea on the board and making it short out.

He could keep that one in his back pocket as a last resort, though.

Rald stepped out onto the bustle of the landing pad with a sigh of relief. Ignoring the shouted order to start unpacking cargo, he leaned his head back to feel the sunshine on his skin. After a week in that hellhole of a ship, he was about to go out of his mind.

Apparently, the crews of the freighters were expected not to fight one another, not even for fun. Not even when the other person really deserved to get their face kicked in.

It was ridiculous.

He wanted a fight, and he wanted a drink. Ignoring yet more shouted orders, Rald picked up his pack and looked around for a transport.

To his surprise, there wasn't one. There was only a dusty road that led to the squalid bunch of buildings that comprised Tethra. The other passengers from the ship—very few, since it was difficult to get clearance to move to this place—had already set off on foot. The road wasn't even paved, and in low places the surrounding swamp flooded it.

There might be eels in the swamp. Rald licked his lips at

the possibility. It had been a while since he'd had a proper eel. Nice and slithery—a true Shrillexian delicacy. No one prepared them correctly, though. They were best served raw. And alive.

If there was no good food to eat in Tethra, he'd come back out here and try his luck.

With a grumble, he hoisted his pack on his shoulder and frowned at the town. This was such a backwater that he wasn't sure what Jutkelon had been doing here. Just because rich people had decided to claim towns in the middle of nowhere it didn't make them good places to do business. What had Jutkelon seen in this place?

When a nearby alien looked at him, Rald realized he'd been muttering aloud.

"It's not much to look at, is it?" the alien offered with a laugh. "But I hear they've got Coke."

"What is…'Coke?'"

"It's a fizzy drink. Humans make it. Damned good." She nodded. "They do some things right, I'll say that."

"Why are you here if you're not a fan of humans?"

"Eh." She lifted her shoulders. "I'm curious, and my uncle was able to bring me here as part of his business. What about you?"

"Just curious too. An old friend lived here. I figured I'd look him up." Rald had a wave of inspiration. "He worked in the mines. Hated it there. Don't know where he is, though."

"Well, if he hated it there you might find him at Aebura's." The alien nodded. "I hear that's a place where they don't like the mines very much."

Rald looked at her curiously.

"There's a division on Devon," she told him frankly. "People who were on top before the humans came in versus people who are on top now. But it's still a fight, and there are still some old grudges. I don't care who wins; I'll work with either. But if your friend didn't like the mine owners, Aebura's is a good place to start looking for him."

"Thank you." Rald managed to force the words out, although his smile was a bit pained. He wished she hadn't been so polite. He would have preferred a good brawl right about now.

But maybe there would be a chance at the bar.

A few minutes and some directions later he slid onto a stool and waited for the bartender to come out.

"Coming!" A woman with blonde hair and warm brown eyes ran out of the kitchen. "Sorry, was just cleaning up. What can I get for you?"

"A Coke, if you have one."

"*Coke* or…" She waited.

"Are there different kinds?"

"Coke it is." She started filling a glass with a dark liquid.

Rald smiled at her. "You Aebura?"

"No, Aebura doesn't run this bar anymore." The woman smiled at him and put down the cup, which was foaming at the top. "My name's Elisa. How about you? New here?"

Rald smiled. "Just here briefly."

But he would be here long enough—long enough to make a lot of people very sorry.

7

Carter perched precariously on a wall at the edge of Tethra and shook the dice. He rolled them onto the wall and groaned as Oemuga hopped with joy.

"Twenty more to me!" The Ubuara gleefully relieved Carter of some of his chips. "Today is not your day, my friend."

Carter shook his head and chuckled. He wanted to get to know his employees and their friends, so he had begun playing dice with the Ubuara during his breaks. Games of pure chance usually weren't his style, but since the Ubuara could sense one another's thoughts those were the only games they ever played.

Luckily, they didn't play for keeps. The set of chips was split at the beginning of the game, and whoever was ahead when everyone stopped won. The games were really just a way for the Ubuara to spend time together.

Carter liked that. When he had come to High Tortuga, the young man in him had been excited by the idea of a town just getting off the ground; full of possibility...and maybe a little bit of danger. He'd lived a long life, but that part of him had never grown old. However, the husband and father in him didn't want his family to be exposed to the type of violence that could be so pervasive in a lot of the less well-charted areas.

Due both to the ethos of the original settlers and to Bethany Anne's growing influence, Tethra was full of possibilities without the sort of desperate rivalries that usually formed in young cities. The citizens seemed to get along well enough, aside from the Luvendi at the edge of town—and they just kept to themselves as far as Carter could tell.

The rest of the citizens seemed happy enough to interact, build businesses together, and spend their free time on games of chance and eel races in the local marsh.

Carter never went to those. There was some mosquito-like thing in those marshes that loved his blood. He was still saving up money for forcefields around all the doors of the bar so he could have a mosquito-free oasis. In the meantime, he hunted the bastards with a single-minded determination that had given him several injuries.

He called them war wounds.

Elisa just rolled her eyes.

Speaking of Elisa, he heard her voice. Carter frowned as he looked around, then pointed to one of the Ubuara on a nearby roof. "Leibura, you want my place?"

The Ubuara chittered and ran down the roof to leap lightly onto the wall. She bared her teeth at him in a tiny grin. "With your luck? You haven't given me much to work with."

Carter laughed as he hopped down. "My apologies. May the dice favor you more than they favored me."

"Now you're wishing *me* bad luck," Oemuga grumbled.

"Never," Carter promised.

He waved to the Ubuara and jogged toward the main street, where he found Elisa looking for him. At the sight of him, she peered curiously down the alley and grinned when she saw the Ubuara.

"Dice again?"

"On a cold streak. That's three games in a row. I'm starting to get nicknames." He looped his arm around her shoulders as they strolled down the street. "Carter the Unlucky. Carter, the Dice's Bitch."

Elisa gave a shriek of laughter. "No Ubuara is going to say something like that."

"Okay, I made that one up. But I promise you, one of these days I will be Carter DiceBane."

"*Very* impressive. I'll have to beat the ladies off you with a stick."

"Could you? I'll probably need a bodyguard. I'm sure I'm going to be quite the celebrity." He smiled as they walked. "It's nice to have these last few days of relative anonymity."

Elisa thumped him on the shoulder and grinned. "Stop it, you'll give yourself too big a head to fit in the door. Anyway, I came to find you for a *reason*."

"Oh. Right. Yes?"

She gave him a look. "There was a Shrillexian in the bar."

"Has he caused trouble?" Carter asked anxiously. "Are you okay?"

"I'm fine. He didn't start a fight and he didn't... You know, it's just kind of weird and I wanted you to know what was going on."

"That *is* weird." Carter considered. "Okay, no more bartending for *you* today."

"Carter." She gave a laugh. "He's gone already."

"Still."

"Stop being so crazy. Look, you can come back and hang out with us if you're worried, but he already left. He doesn't seem to like Coke. He said someone recommended it to him, but he just burped a lot and left without finishing it."

"Yeah, because Pepsi is—"

"Not so loud!" She thumped him again.

"Okay. So he came in and didn't start any trouble? You served him a drink he didn't like and he *still* didn't start anything? *And* he paid for the drink, even though he didn't finish it?" Elisa nodded to all of the questions and Carter shook his head. "You're right. The whole thing reeks of trouble. I don't like peaceful Shrillexians."

"Do you *prefer* them when they're being violent?"

"No, I just really don't like the trouble they bring. Hmm. Well, we'll see if we can get a few Brakalons to just hang out and keep the peace. Aebura might know someone." He shrugged. "You head back—*don't* go in if he's there again—and I'll be there in a moment."

"Okay." She kissed him and jogged away, and Carter hightailed it back to the alley.

"Carter." Leibura gave him a look. "Did you want to come back now that the dice are hot again?"

Carter laughed. "No, this is a very different matter.

Elisa just told me there was a Shrillexian in the bar who was behaving very oddly."

All of the Ubuara took notice. *Everyone* was wary of Shrillexians.

"Anyway," Carter finished, "just keep an eye out, okay? If he does anything weird—or if he heads out of town toward the mine—we should know about it."

As he walked back to the bar he told himself he was being stupid. There were tons of new people on High Tortuga these days. There were probably a bunch of Shrillexians and he just hadn't noticed them.

But for some reason, he couldn't shake the bad feeling he had about this one.

He'd been in good spirits when they'd left Virtue Station, but by the time Fedden got to the cave that served as the base's mess hall he was in a foul mood.

He and Tagurn had landed on Zahal over three hours ago, but a piece of landing equipment had buckled when they set down and they'd spent the time since then fixing it. Fedden was dirty and hungry, and he still didn't have a contract *or* the information he'd wanted to sell.

And their Luvendi contact was taking his sweet time getting here.

He could feel the other ship captains staring at him. Unlike the parts of the syndicate that were planet-based the ships' captains roved all over, taking jobs wherever they could. They came back between jobs to pay the syndicate leaders or just take a break and swap information on potential jobs.

Normally, this suited Fedden. He hated the idea of living on a planet the way Jutkelon had. What if the economy went to shit? What if the mines ran out? Jutkelon had found out the hard way what happened when things changed. On a ship, you could just go somewhere else and find work there.

Theoretically.

Fedden had just been here two days ago, though. Everyone knew he hadn't had time to complete a job since then. He'd been on a cold streak for months, truth be told.

He'd hoped to blow in here, have the Luvendi land within a couple of hours, and head out with a long contract in hand with everyone knowing he'd been the one to find Crallus' precious information, but no such luck.

He glared at the other captains as he sat down. The food was getting worse these days. Crallus was a tight-fisted old bastard, and every year he was talking about raising the buy-in rates for his captains.

He hadn't done it yet, since he knew better than to annoy that many captains at once. But he was greedy, so he was pinching pennies in other ways. The food, for instance, might or might not be packing material. Tagurn poked it with his fork and took a hesitant bite, as though he half-expected to drop dead.

"Struck out, huh?" Namkelon, a Brakalon with skin so deep a gray that it matched the cavern walls, sat down on the other side of the table. When he leaned forward the whole thing tilted.

Fedden grabbed his tray back as it slid toward the

Brakalon. He was in no mood to talk. "Got a client coming to negotiate. Needs more than one crew. Piss me off and I won't recommend you."

"Hey, hey." The Brakalon shook his head. "Things going wrong for you isn't my fault, guy. Anyway, I'm thinking of getting out."

Fedden stopped eating in surprise. "Why?"

"Why do you think? Crallus is talking rate hikes again."

"He always talks rate hikes," Tagurn replied. "He never does it."

"Nah, this time he's gonna. He's got that Torcellan helping him."

"*Which* Torcellan?"

"I don't know. If I knew I'd say, wouldn't I? Some Torcellan. Pale skin." Namkelon shrugged. "Promising him all kinds of shit. Watch your back." He nodded to both of them and stomped off.

Fedden looked toward the roughly-carved ramp at the far end of the room, which led to Crallus' office.

"I don't like this. Crallus sent us off to find information about Devon, and while we're gone he talks more rate hikes?"

"He's not going to pay us for the information," Tagurn predicted. "I bet you anything you get in there and he just takes it as a *favor*. He's got other people who can go get it, so you're only going to get money out of him if he thinks no one else can figure it out."

"What do you know?"

Tagurn leaned forward. "What you *should* know—that Crallus is a piece of shit. He just gets things because he takes them. You want him to give you what you're worth, you gotta take that. Who knows, maybe you don't give him a cut on this job."

"Keep your voice down," Fedden growled.

But he had to admit it was an interesting idea. A *very* interesting idea.

"I'm glad you came to me." Farfaldri Kat poured a cup of tea and handed it elegantly to Rald before sweeping back to his chair to sit.

In the Luvendi custom, he did not have servants to show his wealth. Instead, his surroundings showed it. The floors were of imported stone, the walls were paneled in lacquered wood, and there was cloth draped around the windows.

Rald frowned at that. It actually seemed to be there on purpose, not as a spur-of-the-moment choice.

Well, there was no accounting for taste.

He sipped his tea and tried not to grind his teeth. He needed Kat. Very few people had mentioned anything to do with the mines, and when he mentioned Jutkelon people got a wide-eyed look and shut up hastily.

So he had gone to see Jutkelon's compound—or what was left of it. After almost a month it was still smoking faintly.

That was when Rald had decided he needed more information from people who might have been Jutkelon's allies.

"So what happened at the compound?" he asked. It was too direct a question, but he was getting impatient. He was about to start smashing china, and Kat wasn't going to like that.

"I assume you mean what *kind* of bombs. No one knows." Kat looked displeased. "Everyone there was already dead, however. They were just making a point. And as you can see from the fact that the buildings around it are intact, they made a very *precise* point. I'm told the humans refer to it as 'salting the ground.'"

"So it *was* a human."

"Of course it was a human. Everything that's gone wrong here has been due to humans." Kat shook his head regretfully. "Lan just had the bad luck to be in their sights. I'd have helped him, of course, if it weren't obvious that it would be a futile gesture."

Rald nodded. His mind was racing. "And you don't know the human's name?"

"I do not, but someone at Lan's old mine might. It's owned by the workers now." Kat's tone was so bitter it was a wonder he didn't choke on his words. "I'm sure they know their *hero's* name."

"And if one or two of them suffered you wouldn't mind?" Rald asked. He saw the flash of satisfaction in the Luvendi's eyes and smiled. "Good. I've been wanting a fight. Thank you for your help."

He left, smiling broadly. As he strode toward the edge of town, he noticed one of the large marsh rodents keeping pace with him on a wall. It chittered at him before it bounded up and onto a roof.

Weird place, this. Far too quiet—like a grenade with the pin still in.

Rald was going to fix that.

8

"I'm really not sure about this plan." Gar adjusted his hat nervously.

"*I* think it's hilarious," Shinigami supplied.

"He was talking about its chance of success," Barnabas told her, "not your personal enjoyment. For the record, I also have reservations."

"You're just stuck up. You don't want people to think you'd be someone's assistant."

"I have no qualms about being someone's assistant. *You,* however—" Barnabas broke off. "What was that noise? You said you'd handle landing."

"Did I? I thought you were piloting."

Barnabas swore and took off for the bridge.

Shinigami snickered from the speaker by Gar's ear. "I actually *am* piloting. That noise came from one of the refineries outside. This day has been *fun* so far! I got Barnabas good, and he's got to pretend to be your assistant and do your errands and stuff. Make him do annoying things while you're there, and record it!"

Gar was starting to get used to Shinigami's sense of humor, so he didn't take her too seriously. She and Barnabas liked to poke fun at one another. Shinigami was even starting to get on Gar's case about being too tall, which he understood to be a joke.

He was, however, nervous about this plan. Barnabas was always so calm and collected. Sometimes he ignored the insults people threw at him and his calm nature threw people off. Other times he took the insults *very* seriously, and they realized as soon as they saw his expression that they had overstepped.

Gar had no idea how to do that. When he had spoken with Fedden on Virtue Station he'd been sweating anxiously the whole time, afraid they'd see through his lies and kill him in retaliation.

He was afraid that what made Barnabas so much better than he was at this kind of thing was the knowledge that even if things went south, he'd almost certainly be fine. Gar had *seen* some of what Barnabas could do. He'd seen the human take bullets. Barnabas could rip almost anyone to shreds before they could hurt him, and even if they did, between his durability, healing, and the Pod-docs he'd be fine.

Gar was just going to have to pretend he was like that and trust that Barnabas would have his back out here.

He met Barnabas at the airlock. The human looked disgruntled by Shinigami's trick, but more engaged with the operation than anything else. He was wearing the faraway expression that Gar had learned meant Barnabas and Shinigami were talking silently.

Barnabas nodded in acknowledgment of something Shinigami said.

"Are you ready to go?" Barnabas asked Gar.

"As ready as I'll ever be." Gar ran over the details of his character again and nodded. "Let's go. I want to get in, get the information, and get *out* of there."

Barnabas let the Luvendi precede him down the ramp. At Shinigami's suggestion he had dyed his hair black, the color it had been until a year or so ago, and used contacts to make his eyes brown. She had claimed the hair dye would rinse out quickly, but he was dubious—and he found it strangely jarring to catch glimpses of himself looking like he had in the past.

He had pointed out that aliens were unlikely to be able to differentiate human features very well, and she had pointed out in return that a few big details would therefore be even more likely to deflect them.

He hated it when she was right.

Their Shrillexian contacts were waiting for them at the bottom of the ramp. Fedden seemed deeply displeased about something, though the feeling did not grow when he greeted Gar. Barnabas scanned him quickly and found that the displeasure related to the syndicate.

"Who is this?" Fedden asked roughly. "A *human?*"

"Yes, why?" Gar asked, as if confused that the matter was worthy of comment. He turned to look at Barnabas and did a careful examination. "Is there some problem?"

I have to hand it to him, Barnabas told Shinigami. *He can act.*

Just be careful he doesn't do that with you, Shinigami advised.

77

For now, he's still very uncomfortable when he lies. If that starts to change, I'll know we have a problem.

"He's human," Fedden retorted. "They're the ones who started that shit on Devon." He didn't want anyone here thinking he'd brought in the enemy. His reputation was shaky enough right now.

"I'm not sure if you know this," Gar drew the words out as if speaking to a child, "but there are a *lot* of humans. The ones who made trouble on Devon were part of their government."

Oh, God, he's starting to talk like you. He's telling the truth while he lies.

Don't start.

Fedden looked at Barnabas carefully. "Do any of them have blue eyes?"

"What, humans? I haven't the faintest idea." Gar looked around impatiently. "I don't wish to be rude, but what with concluding our business *and* discussing the matter you wanted help with, we really don't have much time."

Fedden nodded. He gave Barnabas one last narrow-eyed glance but turned away to walk with Gar in a manner that made it clear he considered Barnabas no threat.

Well, look at that. It's working.

It is. Apparently, you were correct about the hair and eye color. Thank you.

I just said to change it, I didn't say to pick colors so unsuited to your looks.

This discussion is over. Actually, no. I'll have you know that I had black hair for years.

Why? It looks terrible.

Okay, now the discussion is definitely over.

Gar followed Fedden through the tunnels to a small cave that had clearly been turned into a conference room. He was surprised to see Fedden set up signal-blockers. Did Fedden realize what they were up to?

Fedden, with one last, suspicious look down the hall-way, closed the door.

"Privacy," was all he said by way of explanation.

Gar did not dare look over at Barnabas. Was there some problem here? Why would Fedden want to block surveillance on his own base?

Gar figured he might as well continue with the plan, since Barnabas had not given him any signals to abort and flee back to the ship. He took the tablet Barnabas held out to him, doing his best to project the aura that he was the most important person in the room. Powerful people generally did that, Barnabas aside. Barnabas' quiet confidence wasn't something Gar could mimic yet.

"Just so we have the particulars out of the way, these are my specifications for the job." He slid the tablet across the table. "Fifty guards—just to start, you understand. We will be expanding. In the meantime, I assure you that other measures will be taken to ensure you're not understaffed. Living quarters will be separated so no larger riots can form, and movement will be...controlled." He smiled the way Lan used to when dealing with people who didn't like to speak openly about the conditions in the mine. "Having been in this business before, I have seen all the tricks. Workers think they're clever, but they rarely are."

Fedden betrayed not a hint of unease. He nodded now and then as he looked over the specifications, and Gar watched him carefully. It was his job to steer the conversation so that Fedden's thoughts would show the things they needed to know. With Barnabas here to interpret those thoughts, they would soon know just what they were dealing with.

"The guards owe me a cut for their work," Fedden told him at last. "I'd appreciate it if that aspect of the payment was handled on your end. Simpler. And it has the added benefit of weeding out the ones who were going to try to pull anything. You wouldn't want them on a work site in any case."

"Indeed." Gar nodded. "Speaking of which, I want to make it clear at the outset that I will take harm to my property very seriously. *Any* of my property." He gave Fedden a hard look.

It was impossible to mistake his meaning, and Barnabas felt a surge of anger when Fedden only smirked and raised an eyebrow. The Shrillexian's thoughts made it *very* clear that he had no intention of complying with this order.

"You have to give them something to do for fun."

"Accommodations will be made." Gar held his eyes. "For the rest, I expect them to ask permission. I will *not* offer forgiveness. Is that clear?"

Fedden stared at Gar, clearly wondering how he meant to enforce this.

Gar did not look at Barnabas, just leaned forward and held Fedden's eyes. "I have ways of making sure that every one of you would deeply regret any such missteps. Again, *is that clear?*"

Fedden looked a bit worried now, and he nodded. Barnabas could feel him re-evaluating his impression of the Luvendi. Fedden was already making mental notes to see if any of his fellow guards had run into Gar before.

That might be a problem. Then again, Barnabas told himself, very few people would know Gar's name. And if Fedden *did* learn who they were, then they could take care of him quickly and quietly before he spread that information around.

"Good." Gar used the trick Shinigami had suggested, changing emotional states quickly enough to cause whiplash. His expression cleared instantly and he reviewed his tablet with a smile. "Now, with proof of the ore coming out of the mines we'll be able to expand quickly. What would be the upper limit you could provide in terms of further guards, and how long would it take them all to travel to us?"

This was one of Barnabas' main questions. This syndicate clearly knew where High Tortuga was. How many of them were there, and where were they? Gar could only hope that the Shrillexian's thoughts betrayed the details.

"I can also have my contacts reach out to them directly if you can give locations," Gar lied smoothly. "We're prepared to offer a buyout on their existing contracts."

Fedden exchanged a look with his second-in-command and Barnabas realized what was happening almost at once. He could have seen it even without reading their thoughts. The look wasn't regarding anything pre-arranged; it had the sense of possibility to it. Gar's question had given them the idea of starting their own syndicate.

In the hallway outside he heard footsteps. Whoever it was—and there were quite a few of them—they were approaching quietly. Between that, Fedden's sudden thought of betraying his syndicate leader, and the signal-canceling devices, Barnabas suddenly had a very bad feeling.

Shinigami, warm up the engines. Passing through the Etheric, his mental speech was not at all impeded by the devices.

Right away. Coming in hot?

We probably will in a few minutes, yes. Any attempted communications out?

None yet.

So this was an internal matter. Barnabas got ready to run and hoped Gar would take instructions well if the whole thing devolved into chaos. In the meantime, he focused on Fedden.

"I can get you between eight hundred and a thousand," Fedden told him. "It'll be a higher rate to me, but it can be done. I'd need some time to arrange it, though."

The door slammed open and another Shrillexian strode into the room. "Because you'd be trying to take my mercenaries?"

Fedden turned his head so guiltily that Barnabas knew he'd been entirely correct in his guesses. Fedden and his second-in-command had been trying to skirt syndicate guidelines, perhaps to avoid giving this other male his cut of the project.

Unfortunately, Fedden's thoughts were now firmly off the subject of the rest of the syndicate's forces or where they were, and unless Barnabas was very much mistaken, Fedden wasn't going to live long enough for them to resume this line of inquiry.

If this were a different situation he'd stay and attempt

to speak to this new Shrillexian, but he had an educated guess as to where this encounter was going. He needed to get Gar out of the mess before the very breakable Luvendi ended up full of stray bullets.

"When I tell you, get down on the floor," he murmured.

Gar gave a tiny nod. His eyes darted around the room, but when the new Shrillexian glanced at him he looked entirely innocent of wrongdoing.

"Is there some problem with this?" he demanded.

"Yeah." The new Shrillexian curled his lip. "He's trying to take over my syndicate."

"Ah," Gar sympathized. "Well, this makes matters rather more complicated." He stood up, still projecting confidence, and swept around the table to deposit a computer chip in the Shrillexian's hand before making his way into the corridor outside. Such was his aura of importance that the mercenaries outside fell back to allow him through. "This has my contact information. I do require quite a sizable number of guards, so whoever is in charge should certainly be in touch when this matter has been resolved."

"Wait." The new Shrillexian pointed at Barnabas. "Who's that? Why d'you have a *human* with you?"

"They have their uses," Gar told him with amusement. "Why is everyone here so interested in him? Do you want to buy his contract?"

For a moment, that seemed to do the trick. In fact, it almost certainly would have—if Fedden hadn't taken that opportunity to shoot the new Shrillexian while his back was turned.

Blood hit the wall of the corridor and Barnabas reacted first. He reached out quietly to take Gar's arm, but forced himself to wait. Gar froze, and so did everyone else in the room.

Then everything descended into chaos. He dragged Gar down the corridor toward the ship, throwing another tiny device into the air to zoom over the heads of the brawlers and seek out the main servers while everyone was distracted.

If they couldn't get the information one way, they'd get it another.

Shinigami, open the door and make sure no one follows us. And since I know you're going to ask—if someone tries, you can use the flamethrower.

Wheeeeeeee!

9

Fedden knew he wasn't likely to get a better chance than this.

Crallus had pissed enough people off by talking about rate hikes that even the Brakalon captains were thinking of leaving. No one liked the new Torcellan, either. Fedden had heard the same whispers from a few people while he'd been back.

It had come to him in a flash. If he took Crallus out now, it was very possible that the rest of the mercenaries would fall in with him instead and accept his leadership.

He hadn't ever particularly *wanted* power. Crallus had power, and what had it gotten him? He clearly hated everything about his life, and without being in the thick of things he was getting soft. He was angry about it, too.

But at that moment a thought came to Fedden and he pulled out his gun. He was sure *he* wouldn't end up that way. Hell, he could live the good life while he was here doing business and then go along with whatever captain he wanted to for a few fights and still keep his edge.

With that vision of the future, the captains would respect him in a way they didn't respect Crallus because Fedden would still be one of them. He would still be a strong fighter—not the strongest, because there was always some young male with something to prove, but strong enough and well respected enough that he wouldn't be as vulnerable as Crallus was now.

His gun came out of its holster so easily that Fedden was *sure* he was doing the right thing. He shivered with excitement.

Which meant the shot went wild. It wasn't *far* off-center. It hit Crallus near the shoulder blade, then there was blood and the other Shrillexian's sudden roar of pain. He crumpled to his knees before anyone moved.

But Fedden knew he'd missed his chance. If he'd taken Crallus out with a single shot he would still have had to sell his takeover, but Crallus would be dead and there would be no reason to fight for him anymore. However, he was still alive and the field was still split.

It was clear that not everyone backed Crallus, but a few of the smarmier captains—the ones who were forever sucking up to him—rushed at Fedden. Crallus had chosen the most loyal of his people to accompany him when he came here to confront the renegade, and Fedden supposed he couldn't fault the bastard for that.

He bared his teeth and yelled as he leapt into action. He knew the rules of this game. Falter for even a moment and he was as good as dead.

So he fought. He fought with everything he had. The first one to charge him was a Brakalon he'd only met a few times. Young and unusually brash for a Brakalon, he had hands the size of Fedden's head.

He was young, though, and prone to the same stupid mistakes all young males made. He charged in too fast and he didn't have any way to arrest his momentum when Fedden stepped forward to meet his charge with a knife to the gut. The Brakalon's eyes went wide in surprise, but before he could react—that wound wouldn't kill him before he could make Fedden sorry—Fedden and the knife were gone.

Another captain was ready for him, however, and as Feddan sidestepped the Brakalon he tackled Fedden straight into a wall. It was a Yofu, his hair shaved off defiantly against the customs of his people. He landed a punch squarely on Fedden's face.

"Traitor!" He drew his hand back for another punch.

Fedden kicked him away. Tagurn was doing nothing to help, the rat. He had hung back and was speaking urgently to one of the other captains as they put pressure on Crallus' wound.

If Fedden survived this he was going to make Tagurn pay for that.

He returned to the Yofu, who was about to come at him again. Fedden sank into a crouch and, when he saw something in his peripheral vision, dove sideways. The Brakalon, now clutching his stomach, stumbled through the space where Fedden should have been. A moment later the Yofu—also unable to course-correct in time—slammed into the Brakalon and bounced off.

Fedden would have grabbed the Yofu by his hair if he'd had any, but instead he cocked an arm as the male stumbled sideways and landed a devastating punch on the Yofu's jaw. Then, not wanting to miss anything where the Brakalon was concerned, he drew his pistol again and put a few shots into the alien's head as the Yofu crumpled to the ground.

The Brakalon went down like a stone, but Fedden had definitely lost this battle in everyone else's mind. Understanding that he would kill them, the rest came at him in a rush. They held down his arms and legs and dragged him out of the conference room and through the corridors.

At some point someone put a sack over Fedden's head, so he was only vaguely aware of where he was being taken. Blows landed on his body and head, and he grunted with pain and struggled. He was going to be killed whenever he got to where he was going, so he might as well make them pay for it.

To his surprise, he found himself in Crallus' office when the hood came off. Crallus was leaking blood and pale with pain, but he knew the importance of appearances. One of the captains was tending him while he sat in his normal chair.

He waved a hand at Fedden. Shoot me if you want, the gesture said, but you didn't kill me when you tried and now you are a captive.

Fedden stared at him wordlessly. What was Crallus going to do? He'd gotten used to thinking of the man as soft and greedy, but he had the sudden vivid memory that Crallus used to have a reputation—the sort of reputation that had made other mercenary captains decide to work with him instead of fighting him. Crallus had been one mean sonofabitch.

Crallus leaned forward. "You wanted my job. You thought you'd kill me and take it. *Ha.*" The laugh caused a bit of blood to leak out of his wound, but he stayed upright. "Not so different from me at that age, Fedden. I respect that. But you killed one of my captains. A good captain; promising. I have to decide what to do with you."

He raised a hand and gestured, and the bag came back down over Fedden's head. He cursed himself as he was dragged away.

Why hadn't he just taken the job with that Luvendi the normal way? He was going to die now.

Records had *not* been kept properly on this planet. Rald hated being stumped by things as trivial as that. He shook his head. Farfaldri Kat had given him good ideas, but it turned out that even the Luvendi could not help Rald determine exactly where the old mines had all been, much less who was there now.

Rald had some ideas of what he might find, of course, but he had survived this long by not assuming his enemies were stupid. These bastards had taken down Jutkelon and the ships' captains. High-impact weaponry had been used on Jutkelon's compound simply to make a point.

He would be foolish to assume that the mine was undefended.

Aebura's had had very few leads, so he had spoken to Kat's head of security and shortly found himself in a bar on the outskirts of the Luvendi district. The bar was packed, mostly with Brakalons. They turned as Rald came in, assessed him indifferently, and went back to their drinks.

Rald looked around as he settled down at the bar and waited to be served. He was about to take a risk.

But he had always enjoyed a good bar fight.

"One of my friends came here a few weeks ago," he announced after his drink had arrived. "Good man. Name of Galagg."

That earned him some narrow-eyed stares.

"He's in the same business as all of us," Rald told them. "Of course, you never got to meet him because a ship named the *Shinigami* shot him down from orbit. Destroyed his ship. His whole crew is dead because some human decided they had a right to tell us what to do on this planet."

He paused to take a sip of the liquid. It was terrible, but at least it wasn't Coke. That stuff had been vile. Full of bubbles.

"Galagg came to help someone you *might* know, though." He raised his glass. "Jutkelon."

There was a pause, then one of the Brakalons at the bar growled, "I knew Jutkelon."

Rald waited, taking another sip of whatever the hell this liquor was. It burned nicely. It would do.

"Ran a good outfit," the Brakalon admitted. He nodded at Rald. "Just a friend of a friend to you, though?"

"We fought together a long time ago," Rald told him. "Sure, he set down on this planet and he didn't fight with me anymore, but we still had each other's backs. Same with Galagg. Maybe I never fought with him, but now that

Jutkelon's dead I figure I'm in this with anyone who wants to help me."

There was a long pause.

"With *what?*" an alien asked. Its wide black eyes blinked at Rald. Taller and more muscled than a Torcellan, its face had a snout-like olfactory organ. It had no ears to speak of.

He wondered briefly what it was and decided he didn't care. He shook his head and looked at each of the people in turn. "I saw what happened to Jutkelon's compound. Now, I won't fault you for not getting involved then. What could you do with that ship in orbit? But it's gone now, and you're just going to let its allies keep what they took?"

A murmur went through the bar. They saw where Rald was going with this.

"Not our problem," one of the Brakalons argued. He shook his head. "I fight for whoever pays me. Jutkelon didn't pay me. Your friend didn't pay me. You don't pay me. You see my dilemma."

Rald had been ready for this. "*No one* is going to pay you if these humans have their way."

There were grumbles around the room, and Rald held the Brakalon's eyes until he looked away.

"I'm searching for their allies," Rald told the group. "And when I know everything there is to know about them, I'm going to go find these humans and turn everything they've tried to do here into a smoking wreck like the one they made of Jutkelon's compound. They wanted to make a point? They thought we'd just sit here and let them do it?" He snorted and his lip curled. "Looking at you, I guess they were right."

They were furious at the insult, but to his surprise they

also looked scared. He understood. They were worried that the humans would come back.

Cowards.

"They're in the other cities," one of the mercenaries informed him shakily. "You *don't* want to fuck with them."

"You're supposed to be mercenaries!" Rald spat contemptuously. "No one's supposed to want to fuck with *you*. You start getting weak like this—just roll over and let people take whatever they want, let them kill your friends without fear of your revenge—and what *are* you? Not a mercenary anymore, *that's* for sure. You don't even have any pride left."

"You think you can win if you go up against them?" One of the mercenaries shook his head. "You're wrong. No one knows all their capabilities."

"Which is why we start with information," Rald told him. "So tell me what you know of the humans here. There are some at that bar, Aebura's."

The black-eyed alien made a hissing noise. "Friends of the Ubuara. Those little rats, you know? The one who runs it—he fought with them at the mines."

Rald signaled for the barkeeper to refill the alien's drink. "Tell me about him. Tell me about his mate, too. And his young."

10

"That went better than I expected," Barnabas announced, mostly to himself. The *Shinigami* banked smoothly away from Zahal, taking a very direct route out of the atmosphere and away from any anti-aircraft measures.

Gar looked at him. "Sarcasm?"

"Not at all. We learned how many of them there might be, which is considerably more than I thought there were. That is unfortunate, certainly. But we were able to get the interior layout of the base and a scan of security measures they have in place, and that crawler should find their main communications hub soon so we can tap into it."

Barnabas headed toward his rooms as he spoke. He paused at the door of the suite and turned to give Gar a smile. "I'll be back shortly."

"You don't want to debrief now?" Usually, Barnabas put business before relaxation.

"I want to wash this hair dye out immediately," Barnabas explained. "I do not like it at all. Not a *word*," he added in the direction of the nearest speaker and disappeared into his rooms.

Gar headed back into the main seating area and paced around the outside of it. No matter how much Barnabas and Shinigami tried to ignore it, the fact remained that Gar really had nothing to offer them except the fact that he was Luvendi. He was able to approach people who might not speak to a human.

A crew member should offer more than that. Of course, Gar knew the real reason he was here, but in the long run, it was going to be awkward for everyone if he could not bring anything at all to the table.

What did he have as a Luvendi?

He stopped. He actually *did* have something useful.

"Shinigami, would you bring up the files we extracted from Lan's computers?"

There was a pause and Gar assumed Shinigami was asking Barnabas what he thought of the request, but a moment later one of the screens obligingly populated.

Gar sat down, tablet in hand, and began searching and making notes. He did not know very much about fighting, it was true. However, being Luvendi meant he had long ago learned to solve problems *without* fighting. A Luvendi out and about in the galaxy had to learn to defuse tense situations and achieve goals without physical violence.

Until recently, Gar had taken a lot of pride in his ability to do just that. Nonetheless, since joining Barnabas aboard the *Shinigami* he had become frustrated with how round-about his own methods were. Barnabas tended to solve problems very directly, while Gar simply could not.

Now his roundabout methods might be able to help.

Gar was still deep in his research when Barnabas came back into the room. His hair was not precisely its former color, although it was close, and his eyes were back to blue. Gar wondered how he had changed the eye color but decided not to ask. Though most species seemed to have only a single pupil in their eyes, Gar had never gotten used to the appearance of it. He tried to avoid thinking about other species' eyes, in fact. He shuddered slightly.

"What are you looking at?" Barnabas asked curiously.

"Lists of the Luvendi I know who are part of the company your Empress bought. Luvendan itself is large, but Luvendi who are out in the wider universe tend to know one another. There aren't very many of us. I knew some, and Lan knew some others."

Barnabas looked at the screen, then raised an eyebrow to ask for clarification.

"Luvendi tend to manage things," Gar explained. "We handle the details of other people's businesses because we can't do manual labor. The ones who have found jobs off Luvendan are *very* good at it. Lan ran quite a profitable mine, for instance. Before I worked for him, I managed an information broker's staff."

"What's your point?"

"My point is that the Luvendi could be a good asset to you. Getting the cooperation of a Luvendi in any of the businesses you're looking at would mean we would get the inside information about their cash flow, their associates, and their locations—everything. That's the first thing."

"And the second thing?" Barnabas took a seat and propped his elbows on his knees. To Gar's relief, he seemed interested instead of dismissive.

"From word of mouth and, well...knowing Lan, I can tell which of these people might be involved in shady things. Things your Empress—"

"She's not the empress anymore," Barnabas murmured.

Gar scowled in annoyance. "It's not the Empire anymore, and you're not a Ranger. You all say things like that, but you haven't given me any other terms to work with."

"Well, the Federation—"

"He has a point," Shinigami interrupted. "I've taken to calling you 'Vigilante One.'" Barnabas frowned. "You knew what he meant anyway," Shinigami stated flatly. "Ignore him, Gar. Tell us more about your shady friends."

"They're not my friends."

"They're people you would have associated with before meeting me," Barnabas reminded him.

"Yes." Gar held his tongue rather than justify his earlier actions. "There is a difference between a business associate and a friend, however. These people were my rivals. They would think they still are if I were to contact them. We were all competing for the most lucrative jobs."

"Whilst ignoring the effects those jobs had on others."

Again Gar held his tongue, answering with a simple, "Yes."

Barnabas thought Stephen would be impressed. When Barnabas had first met Gar and the Luvendi had run from him Barnabas had held him in complete contempt, but even in the first meeting he had seen something unusual in Gar.

He was willing to face his past mistakes. He did not protest or make excuses.

It was one of the reasons Barnabas believed Gar could atone for his past wrongs.

"Have you heard of Stephen?" he asked Gar.

"I...have not, no."

"He is another like me, from Earth. Those with our abilities had a familial structure. We would pass those abilities to 'children' who were not of our lineage, but chosen due to their characters. We were responsible for their actions, so we tried to select carefully. Stephen made some mistakes when he chose, and his first meeting with Bethany Anne was...unpleasant. Now he is one of the first among her friends." Barnabas smiled slightly. "Gar, a person can move beyond their mistakes and become something greater, but they must *reflect* on those mistakes, not simply admit to them. They must understand why they made them and what they will change to avoid them in the future."

Gar frowned. He was not entirely sure where this was going.

"You are so eager to figure out what you want to do that you are ignoring what you were," Barnabas told him. "You want to prove yourself, so you are trying to mold yourself into anything and everything you think might be..." He paused and smiled wryly. "Sufficient to save your life, if I'm guessing correctly."

"Yes," Gar admitted. He swallowed nervously.

"Stephen let his children run roughshod because they were his weakness," Barnabas explained. "He loved each of them and that love led him to look the other way rather than fight them. Even when he knew they were wrong, he did not do what he should have to stop them. Though he is now a very different person in some ways, that care for his family still remains. Do you see?"

"I...don't think I do."

"Even *I* don't," Shinigami concurred.

Barnabas looked annoyed at her interjection, but when he looked at Gar again, it was with practiced good humor.

"You have good qualities," he told Gar bluntly. "Both good qualities and bad can lead to mistakes. If you want to rebuild yourself into a different kind of person, into the kind of person who could be an ally of mine, then you must capitalize on your good qualities to keep the bad in check. It is a choice you will make every day; every time there is the chance to do the wrong or easier thing."

Gar hesitated, then nodded.

"You have shown creativity," Barnabas explained. "Today, for instance, you drew on your knowledge of other Luvendi to get information from these files that neither Shinigami nor I could have extracted. You have shown an ability to read the people you talk to and elicit information from them. In the past, your cowardice led you to use these skills to get ahead, no matter what the cost."

"I thought that everyone was just out for themselves," Gar admitted quietly. "That everyone would screw one another over given the opportunity. I thought I should just play the game as well as I could, and that the people I took advantage of would not be upset because I was doing the same thing they would in my place. I valued my physical safety above all else."

"And now?" Barnabas asked.

"Now I think I have made some terrible mistakes." Gar hung his head in shame. "When I let Lan shoot me, I did so because it was more important to me to confront him than it was to be safe. In retrospect, that seems terribly foolish."

"Confronting injustice is never foolish," Barnabas told him gravely. Then, seeing Gar's solemn face, he winked. "Though I *would* invest in a bulletproof vest if you intend to do that often."

Gar chuckled. "They showed me there was another way." His spine straightened again. "On High Tortuga. The mine workers took risks for one another. It was the complete opposite of anything I had ever experienced. It made so little sense to me that I did not even perceive it as something which could happen. I would like to fight for something like they fought for their freedom, but I don't know what I want to fight for."

"It's a good start." Barnabas nodded. "A very good start. You say these people aren't friends? Lan wasn't your friend. You've kept yourself apart from everything for a long time, Gar. I think if you stop doing that, you'll find something you want to fight for."

He smiled and left Gar to his thoughts and his research.

Don't you want to debrief?

We can do it later. Barnabas made his way to the bridge. Between Shinigami's piloting capabilities and the fact that they had yet to engage in a ship-to-ship conflict together, Barnabas was rarely in that location.

He was not sure what had brought him here now. He wandered around the room, hands in his pockets, inspecting the computer terminals and the captain's chair.

Could I make an observation? Shinigami asked.

It depends on whether you intend to be snarky.

It's not snark. She waited a moment. *I don't think that*

speech back there was all for Gar. I think some of it was what you *needed to hear.*

I like to think I already have a very well-tuned moral compass, thank you. And a good grasp of my strengths and weaknesses.

No, you don't. All right, the morals I'll give you. But when was the last time you let someone in?

Tabitha. Barnabas settled into the captain's chair. *A bizarre choice.*

You know that's not true. And yes, you did let her in. And Bethany Anne, and some of the rest. But they were all part of... something more. You didn't have to let your guard down in the same way. You could be a part of the group. When it's not like that, you hold yourself apart just as much as Gar does.

I do not. What about Carter? Aebura?

People you left behind on the planet with a smile and a wave. You should set up a weekly game night with Carter. See? When I said that you looked really uncomfortable.

Barnabas stood up again and glared at nothing in particular. It was annoying to argue with Shinigami. He never knew where to direct his expressions.

And what about Sarah? Shinigami asked finally.

Barnabas went still. He swallowed. He wasn't even sure how Shinigami knew about Sarah. Who had mentioned her?

What about her?

You know exactly what I mean, Shinigami told him. *I don't know a ton about humans, but I know what you looked like when you came in here, and that's lonely. You miss Tabitha and the rest of them.*

I had to come out here on my own. It was what I needed to do.

Shinigami hesitated for a long moment before she spoke again. *You need other people too, or you'll lose sight of what you're fighting for.*

11

Tagurn was sweating nervously.

He knew Fedden was furious with him, and he hoped that whatever happened he'd be able to explain what was going on. Tagurn hadn't meant to be disloyal. He didn't like Crallus very much, and he *definitely* didn't like the new second-in-command.

Or whatever that Torcellan was. Tagurn could just see the pale hands. The being made sure his face was well shadowed and he sat in a chair at the corner of the room, as self-possessed as if he were the one running everything.

Maybe he was. Tagurn could see Crallus working not to look over his shoulder. Was he nervous? Was he waiting for the Torcellan's approval of his plans?

It didn't matter very much. All that mattered was getting Fedden out of this alive. Tagurn had known as soon as the shot went wild that Fedden's only chance of survival was to have someone speaking on his behalf. If they both launched themselves into the fight, it would turn into a brawl and people were likely to die, Fedden and Tagurn included.

However, if it was just one fighter, people might hang back.

So Tagurn had gone to speak to Crallus, and he'd heard the boss's assessment: challenges weren't personal, they were just part of the business, but Fedden had shown he wasn't to be trusted with the lives of the ships' captains. He would have to pay.

And now they'd called Tagurn here.

He linked his hands behind his back and forced himself to meet Crallus' eyes. He would get nowhere by being deferential. Deference was a weakness. Tagurn needed to argue his point.

But what *was* his point?

"Tell us about the human and the Luvendi," the Torcellan prompted.

"We met the Luvendi on Virtue Station. He told us he'd had his mine shut down on Devon." Tagurn looked only at Crallus as he answered. *Are you really in charge here?*

Perhaps in answer, Crallus looked back at the Torcellan. He winced as he did so. The wound had been stabilized, but no technology the syndicate had on Zahal could heal a bullet hole so quickly.

"What were their names?" the Torcellan pressed. "What was their ship?"

"We were not told the human's name. I assumed it was not important since he was treated as a very junior associate." It was difficult to know if his words were being well received with the Torcellan's face hidden in shadow. The alien had leaned back, finally. Though he was looking toward Tagurn, there was no way to know his expression.

For all Tagurn knew he was digging himself into a massive hole.

The Torcellan's reply was carefully neutral. "You assumed it was not important."

Tagurn's heart sank. This was not a good sign. "Yes."

"You were sent to find information about what happened on Devon, an event that is tied directly to a human presence there, and you did not ask for more information about a human you *knew* had been on the planet?"

"We didn't know if *he*... He might have been hired..." Tagurn stuttered to a stop and let his head drop. There were too many failures for him to rectify. He had come in here intending to talk about Fedden challenging Crallus and instead they were talking about the information from Devon.

He wasn't sure why it was so damned important. Mercenaries died all the time. Mercenaries who died because they underestimated their opponents weren't worth avenging; they were a dead weight that had been cut off.

You were better off without someone like that on your team.

"Perhaps you think this issue is not worthy of your attention?" the Torcellan asked. He was eerily perceptive.

Tagurn fought the urge to flee.

"You would be wrong," Crallus told him. After his silence so far the low growl of his voice surprised Tagurn. "What happened on Devon is part of a much larger event. It threatens...wider interests."

The Torcellan made a faint hissing noise and Crallus stopped talking. So he wasn't a second-in-command at all, Tagurn realized. He was in charge, somehow. This just kept getting worse.

Tagurn gathered all his courage and looked at Crallus, then at the Torcellan. "What can we do to make this right?"

There was a pause. "'We?'" the Torcellan echoed.

"Fedden. Me." Tagurn's hands clenched.

"You're sticking with him, then?" Crallus' face was unreadable.

Tagurn should run. He knew that. He should ask to join another crew, beg for another chance after having tainted his reputation by even being associated with Fedden. To his surprise, though, he found he wasn't willing to do that.

"He is my captain and my friend," Tagurn told them. Then, because he realized that if they were going to kill him the decision was already made, he added, "You're angry that he killed another captain, but that captain was trying to kill *him*. I know how it started, but you said yourself that challenges are part of this life."

To his surprise, Crallus smiled. It was not a *nice* smile, but it didn't promise death and retribution, either. "I did say that," the syndicate leader agreed. "That's how I took over. He did it in public. He didn't try to sneak around. I can respect that."

The Torcellan made a faint disgusted noise. "We do not have time for this. Shrillexian, you asked what you could do to make this right."

Crallus and Tagurn exchanged a look and Tagurn's curiosity deepened. This Torcellan seemed to know nothing and care for nothing about their life, but Crallus was listening to him. Crallus didn't seem to care much about the humans on Devon. He had never been one to bow and scrape to other people. Hell, he told even their richest clients to fuck off if they got annoying.

Why the hell was he listening now? Why was he sending his captains to collect information, and why had he mentioned "wider interests?"

Crallus said nothing now, and Tagurn realized that even he did not know what the Torcellan was going to say. What the hell was going on here?

"We have a name," the Torcellan informed them. "The ship that took down ours was almost certainly the *Shinigami*. It's a human ship associated with...whatever the humans call themselves now. A Federation, apparently." He waved a hand dismissively. "We have heard whispers that a Ranger was involved—not Ranger Two, the one many people know about, but Ranger One. This is unconfirmed, but if it happens to be true... Well, let us simply say that many people would be happy to have such a menace removed."

Tagurn swallowed. He was pretty sure he knew where this was going.

"Normally, the person who took down this ship and this human could expect great renown," the Torcellan continued. "They would be a hero—or whatever you people call someone who defends the group. Do mercenaries even have a word for that?"

The contempt was so sudden and so thick that even Crallus tensed.

"We are not animals," the syndicate leader protested.

"We defend our own. Why do you think the ships went to Devon in the first place?"

The Torcellan lifted an ambivalent shoulder. He seemed unconvinced of any higher motive beyond a propensity for violence.

"As I mentioned, such a one would ordinarily expect riches beyond their wildest dreams. Fame. That one could expect to be honored. But *you* can expect much more, Tagurn. Much more even than that."

Tagurn frowned.

"You," the Torcellan told him, "can expect to be *forgiven*." There was a silence. "Do you not understand? That is how completely you have failed. The kind of extraordinary deed that would normally bring you wealth, fame, and a fleet of your own—all of that is needed simply to bring you back to zero."

Tagurn's heart almost stopped.

"And yet you will be permitted to redeem yourself," the Torcellan continued beatifically. "Is this not wonderful news?"

Before a week ago I didn't even know you existed, Tagurn wanted to say. Crallus doesn't seem to know what you're going for. Why the hell should I care whether you think I've redeemed myself?

He did not say it. Something in the Torcellan's tone and in the way he had come in here and simply expected Crallus' obedience hinted at larger events in play. Events Tagurn could not comprehend.

He had spent years as a mercenary, fighting for people who wanted to take anything they laid their eyes on. Those people wanted to be feared, but Tagurn hadn't feared them. Without mercenaries on their side they were nothing.

For the first time though, he had the sense that the universe was larger than he knew. That there were people he had never heard of who cared about what he did, and who could crush him like a bug if he displeased them.

It terrified him.

"May I go get Fedden?" he asked.

The Torcellan sank back in his seat with a faint air of disappointment, but Crallus nodded.

"Go. Get him. Find the *Shinigami* and kill the human."

"There will need to be proof," the Torcellan murmured. "And the ship, itself, Tagurn. Do not forget to bring that back. There is something aboard that we need."

"What?" Tagurn could not keep himself from asking.

"One of their AIs. We have not yet managed to capture one. Once it is ours… Well, it is of no consequence to you. Go. Redeem yourself." The Torcellan nodded to Crallus. "We have come across some information that will help you find allies. The human killed two Luvendi—Venfirdri Lan and Venfaldri Gar. Proof of this may help you. You see, we are not cruel. We are giving you a chance to succeed."

Venfaldri Gar? *No.* It couldn't be.

But there was no mistaking it.

No. Oh, no. They were so fucking screwed.

"One other thing," the Torcellan added. His voice was pleasant, but it somehow also turned Tagurn's blood to ice. "We have several other individuals now searching for the ship and its captain. You will only be absolved if you find it first."

Tagurn managed to keep his face straight as he ducked

his head and hurried out of the room, but as soon as he was in the corridor he ran as if he were being chased by a pack of bloodthirsty *ekthoya*.

He practically skidded into the brig, to find that Fedden was already being released. The other Shrillexian bared his teeth at Tagurn. "Get out of my sight."

"We have to leave. Right now." Tagurn shook his head, and when Fedden only glared at him he grabbed his captain by the arm and dragged him into a corner. "I'll explain what I did later, and if you still want to kill me you're welcome to try. But right now we have to get out of here. You will die if you don't. Every second we're here is a risk."

Fedden didn't look any friendlier, but whatever he saw in Tagurn's face, he didn't argue.

They strode through the halls with the back of Tagurn's neck prickling. Every fiber of his being was consumed with the desperate hope that they could kill the human and rectify their mistake.

Before that damned Torcellan learned that they'd had two chances at the *Shinigami* and missed them both.

12

At least once every day when he thought no one was looking, Barnabas snuck away to a corner of the ship to sit quietly by himself.

Shinigami tried not to interrupt him when he did this. It was such a quintessentially human thing to do, to forget that she was an AI and was omnipresent on this ship. There were no private places.

At first, she had been fascinated. What was he doing? She analyzed his vital signs and found that his heartbeat slowed and his breathing became deep and even. He was not sleeping, however. His brain activity was off the charts. Some days it seemed to be pure thought, and other days a tangle of emotion so bright that Shinigami was surprised he wasn't laughing hysterically—or smashing the ship to pieces with his bare hands.

Later, she decided that simply not announcing her presence wasn't enough. She would turn off her cameras whenever he went to be alone, and she would wait until he moved somewhere else in the ship to turn them back on.

Now, however, she was fairly sure she needed to disturb him. She knew where he was—in a small alcove in one of the corridors, where a window showed the vast blackness outside. Today there was a particularly pretty cluster of stars visible from that window, one bluish and one a reddish-orange color.

"Barnabas?" She projected her voice out of a speaker a little way down the corridor.

The sensors there recorded him moving around and then he came around the curve of the corridor curiously. "Shinigami?"

"I'm sorry to disturb you," Shinigami apologized. "It's about the server data from the syndicate."

Barnabas frowned. "Why did you not speak directly to me where I was?"

Shinigami hesitated. She had so much data on human minds, but much of it was contradictory or illogical or both. She had no idea how Barnabas was going to respond to the truth. However...

"When you come down here to sit alone, I turn off my cameras and speakers so you have privacy."

There was a pause. Barnabas said nothing for a long moment. By the standards of how fast both he and Shinigami thought, a *very* long moment.

"Thank you," he murmured at last.

Shinigami was surprised by the depth of emotion in his voice. She looked for the signs of anger and found them deep below, as always, but the anger did not seem to be directed at her. There was also a hint of strain in his features that conveyed sadness.

She wanted to ask him what he had been thinking

about, but was not sure she should. After all, he could have spoken to her if he had wanted to do so. Instead, he had gone to be alone.

"What did you want to tell me?" he asked finally. His face had cleared. Whatever his turmoil was, he had set it aside for now.

"The crawler found its way into their communications hub and managed to get the data out to us. What I'm looking at suggests this is a *much* bigger operation than we thought."

"I'll come up to the conference room."

Barnabas made his way through the corridors quickly. "Start at the beginning. You said 'suggests?'"

"It's a fairly standard set-up for mercenary groups. They're pretty independent, and they give a cut of their take to the syndicate leader. In this case, it's a Shrillexian named Crallus. It's very decentralized. They have the base here, and a larger one in a different system."

"Should we head there?"

"Not right now. The syndicate leader was there when you met with Fedden."

"Fedden shot him. It's why we left so quickly. Is he still alive?"

"I haven't seen any communications that would suggest otherwise." Shinigami paused and Barnabas imagined her shrugging. "In any case, the other hideout is well-defended in terms of *automated* defenses, but it's not the main stopping point for any of their ships. We could smash it, but it wouldn't do us much good."

"Shinigami, you're telling me that there is a large base that we could expend significant time and effort smashing to smithereens, with a lot of—what was it you called them?"

"Pretty explosions!"

"Yes. Pretty explosions." Barnabas, who had always thought 'pretty' was supposed to refer to women, flowers, and unicorns, tried to keep his face straight. "In any case, now you're advocating that we do *not* do this? I think that might be personal growth."

"I said not right *now*. If at some point our path takes us through that system and you want to make a little detour and have some fun? I wouldn't complain."

"Add a bottle of wine and a movie and you have a nice evening," Barnabas commented.

"You and Stephen must have very similar taste in women." Shinigami waited for the laughter and was surprised instead to see a sad expression cross Barnabas' face. On a hunch, she switched to a scan and saw an echo, very faint, of the turmoil she had seen in him when they first began talking.

She had a memory of mentioning Sarah to him, and she suddenly remembered the story Tabitha had told her about Barnabas' past—a story the irreverent, terminally sarcastic Tabitha had told very solemnly.

The expression was gone in an instant, however, and she had the sense that Barnabas didn't want to speak of it.

She switched the subject instead. "There's not much at the base. Crallus only goes there sometimes. It was really set up by the person he took over from. Hard to tell who that was since he didn't do much in the way of his own paperwork. Real old-school robber-baron."

Barnabas grimaced. "And Crallus was his protégé?"

"It's not something that shows up in any of their documentation, but let's just say that Crallus took over very suddenly."

"Ah, the other kind of transfer of power, then." Barnabas smiled tightly. He didn't feel particularly sorry for Crallus' predecessor. Mercenary syndicates were almost stereotypical in their propensity for this sort of thing. It was just what happened when you got a lot of people in one place who all made their living by killing for money. Of the people who ran mercenary groups, not very many ended up dying of old age.

"Pretty much," Shinigami agreed. "He isn't super-important, *except* that he got the group hooked into something called 'the Yennai Corporation.'"

Barnabas let his eyes drift closed for a moment. He already knew what Shinigami was going to say, or at least, the rough shape of it. He'd seen enough of the universe to know that much.

"Let me guess. The Yennai Corporation isn't part of any particular industry. Its tendrils are hooked into almost anything you can think of."

"That's about the size of it. So far I've tracked mentions of them to legal, semi-legal, and illegal weapons and drug trafficking, transport—that would be cargo *and* people—a few mercenary syndicates like this one, banking, some information brokers, agriculture, mining, station parts manufacturing, pharmaceuticals—"

"I'm going to stop you for a moment." Barnabas held up a hand. "Would it just be quicker to say that pretty much wherever we go and whoever we interact with, we can assume word might get back to them?"

"Yes, probably. I was just impressed by how successful they had been so far."

"Corporations like this tend to be." Barnabas shook his head and began to scroll through the information on the screens. "Like Crallus' organization, it's organic. They allow the syndicates a *lot* of leeway. They don't waste resources overseeing after they give the initial cash infusion. They just let the cut trickle up to them, along with any information these people are able to provide. When things get going, that means they know all the emerging markets and also have a very good idea of where threats might emerge."

Shinigami considered this. "I'm going to hazard a guess that we count as threats."

"Your analytical algorithms really are top-notch."

"Sarcasm? Really? When I just found us all this information?"

"That wasn't very sporting of me. I apologize." Barnabas paused at one and sighed. "So, the bankers I spoke with on Virtue Station?"

"Ah, yes. Yennai has contacts in all those banks, as well as the company that provides security for the station *and* the company that built the station in the first place. I'd say someone from there has probably already read a brief about what went down while we were there. In fact, now that I think of it, it's probably why Mustafee Boreir disappeared."

Barnabas sighed and ran a hand through his hair. "And we weren't cloaking who we were when we went there, either."

"No, we weren't." Shinigami sounded cautious. "Should I have?"

"I didn't ask you to." He sat on the edge of one of the tables and stared into the middle distance. "Well, *this* might get interesting."

"Explain."

Barnabas cleared his throat as he considered. "When we started this quest I thought we were tracking down the dregs of the corporation Bethany Anne bought out—a few disaffected employees, that sort of thing. That was what we had with Lan. Then I figured, well, the mercenary groups that were on the planet probably tended to look for planets like that. I thought we would just organically track our way through various groups who would have known about High Tortuga and might have had a grudge. After all, you did all that good research on people who might have."

Shinigami was quietly pleased. Barnabas did not give praise unless he thought it was merited. However, she saw that Barnabas now looked troubled. He pushed himself up and began to pace, running his hands through his hair again. "I don't like hiding. I don't *like* skulking around and giving fake names unless there's a very specific purpose to it, like with Fedden. If my reputation precedes me, all the better."

At last Shinigami understood. "But now we've pissed off someone we might not be able to take on by ourselves."

Barnabas nodded. He crossed his arms and looked at the screens.

"Well, then maybe we consider this to be a good and very specific reason to sneak around," Shinigami suggested after a moment.

"Mmm." Barnabas still didn't seem entirely pleased by this, in her opinion.

"I mean, it's not completely bad," she told him. "We found a gigantic corporation with hundreds of shadowy tentacles all over known space. We're pretty outmatched."

"I think your language couplings might be experiencing a malfunction. Or your reasoning modules." Barnabas frowned at one of the cameras. "Other than the fact that we know their name, it *is* completely bad."

A sniff came from the speaker closest to Barnabas. "I don't think so. Hell, you shouldn't think so, either."

Barnabas allowed a smile to slip out. He figured this was probably a joke, but he was enjoying Shinigami's sense of humor. "Would you care to explain?" he asked with exaggerated courtesy. He sat in one of the chairs and nodded for her to continue.

"We haven't known each other for very long," Shinigami began hesitantly, "so I might be *way* off on this as a personal assessment. However, there are a couple of things I've noticed about you. First, of the seven deadly sins, yours would be pride."

"I beg your pardon?"

"You heard me. And second, you really like being sneaky."

Barnabas raised an eyebrow at the camera. "I assume there's a point to all this?"

"Oh, there is, and it's this: we're up against someone who can call on overwhelming force and might just do so if you piss them off enough. They've got virtually unlimited resources at their disposal. How satisfying would it be to set up a series of traps that result in you razing this company to the ground? They'll never in a million years imagine that one human in one ship could do that."

Barnabas sat very still.

"You don't want to admit I'm right," Shinigami gloated. "But you would just *love* that. One man taking down this whole rotten corporation. Of course, it would be impossible without his partner in crime, the Dread Ship *Shinigami*."

Barnabas' lips quirked, but he went to the heart of the matter rather than tease her about the name. "We don't know it's *all* rotten. We should really do our due diligence—"

"Oh, come on, we totally know."

"Yes, we do. All right, I admit it. You're right. About all of it. Don't tell anyone."

"That you're proud of your sneakiness? *Everyone* knows."

"We'll get back to that. After I've taken down the Yennai Corporation. *In the meantime,* I suggest we— What was that?" There was a beeping noise from the speakers.

"Someone's shooting at us," Shinigami reported. "They all just appeared out of nowhere."

"*All?*"

"There are four of them. Wait, five. No… Look, there are a lot of them, okay? Get to the bridge and I'll start evasive maneuvers. And tell Gar to strap in. We might have to do some barrel rolls."

13

E rgix Koyissa Get'ruz III, captain of the YCS *Get'ruz*, checked the position of the other ships in the formation and gave a decisive nod.

"Begin the standard capture sequence and broadcast a message across all Yennai channels to stay out of our way."

He had started Get'ruz Shipping decades ago using the money he'd made after hijacking a cargo vessel full of nutritional algae and selling the cargo. The ship and crew he had used to start his own fleet of cargo vessels.

His philosophy was very simple. Shipping was dangerous, and unprotected ships were liable to be stolen—by him. Anyone who worked for him could take any ship they wanted, after which they were responsible for maintenance, cargo contracts, and security to keep it from getting stolen again. In return, they got to distribute the goods and keep whatever profits they could.

Ergix provided backup and negotiation when the people he'd stolen from got uppity, and now he sat at the center of a tidy little shipping empire.

It was an empire, however, that had once been close to collapsing. A captain, too young and inexperienced to know what he could and couldn't get away with, had stolen a ship full of ore meant for the Jotun government's shipyards and their Imperial Fleet had gotten involved.

The Jotun bastards might look like bags of jelly and they might keep mostly to themselves, but it had turned out to be a mistake to underestimate them. The bags of jelly had fine-tuned the practice of creating power suits for themselves and they also had a fleet of ships that were some of the most advanced in the universe—and Ergix' damn-fool captain had fled directly back to headquarters with that fleet on his ass.

Which was where Yennai Corporation had stepped in. Just when Ergix was sure he was done for, a few slim, agile ships had appeared between his base and the Jotun fleet. An encrypted conversation had ensued, and the Jotun fleet had dispersed without so much as a goodbye.

The Yennai Corporation's representatives had then offered Ergix and his ships membership. "Surely he could see the benefits of being part of their organization?" they had asked.

He could.

The thing was, they didn't even ask for very much. Ergix sent a relatively minor cut of his income to them, passed along any news he thought was of note, and occasionally handled targets or provided security at their request. They never got in his face about how he ran Get'ruz, either.

So when they said jump, he jumped—like right now, keeping an eye out for any human ship registered to the former Etheric Empire. He'd staked out the main routes leading away from where they had last been seen, and it hadn't been long before they had dropped into his lap.

"Sir." Helix, his niece and one of the junior communications officers aboard Ergix's flagship, swung around in her chair. "We're being hailed by another Yennai-affiliated ship. It asks to be involved in the capture and reports that it is one hour away."

Ergix stared at her incredulously. "An *hour*? It wants us to keep this ship on the line but not capture it for an *hour* while it gets here? No. Close communications from it and give the information to Jeryx so he can keep an eye out for it. Whoever they are, we don't need them interfering."

"Yes, sir." She relayed the message and then pulled the earpiece away from her head with a wince. "He wants to speak to you, sir. He says it's urgent."

"No," Ergix repeated. "I don't care what he wants. This was an Etheric Empire ship. The only way we're taking it is with the element of surprise. Keeping it on the hook for an hour is not an option. Shut down communications and focus on the operation."

"Yes, sir."

"Request denied," said the female voice from the *Get'ruz*. "Communications are hereby terminated."

On the bridge of his ship, Fedden slammed his hand down and snarled in fury and desperation.

He *had* to be there when they captured the ship. *He had to be involved.* Tagurn, who was never worried by the people in charge, had been afraid of what this Torcellan might do—and Tagurn's instincts had helped Fedden steer clear of innumerable bad decisions.

Fedden was one mistake away from being an example to the rest of Crallus' organization, and he knew it.

"Throw everything at this," he told Tagurn. "I don't care what safety protocols you have to ignore to get us there in time, just *do* it."

Tagurn, for once, did not argue.

He knew as well as Fedden did that it was no use surviving the trip if they failed to take the *Shinigami.*

"All passengers, please take your seats and brace for impact," Shinigami announced in an artificially pleasant tone.

"Impact?" Barnabas strapped himself into the captain's chair, then glanced at the speakers. "Shinigami—*impact?*"

"It's only wise to be cautious." She was still using the tone Barnabas remembered from airline stewardesses back on Earth.

It made his teeth ache. That had been one of the worst things about flying. "Please stop talking like that."

In answer, Shinigami sent the ship into a barrel roll. Barnabas closed his eyes as his body pressed against the straps of the harness.

"Was that really necessary? What about Gar?"

"Gar is better off if the ship doesn't get captured," Shinigami replied breezily. "And yes, it was necessary.

They're not trying to shoot us down, they're trying to capture the ship."

"Oh, really?" Barnabas lifted an eyebrow. "That's a surprise. A convenient one, I'd say."

"Why? Are you thinking what I'm thinking?"

"If what you're thinking is that this gives us an excellent chance to shoot them all down while they're focusing on capturing us in one piece, then yes." Barnabas gave a small satisfied smile. In a direct battle the name of the game was simple—take the other side down.

Weapons would have been used immediately if their attackers had not wanted to capture them. However, they had not, and they were now at a disadvantage. Shinigami could use weapons and they could not.

They would break eventually, of course. It would become too costly to keep trying to capture a ship that was taking down their fleet. In the meantime, their tacticians would be occupied by trying to maneuver into position both to capture the ship and avoid missiles, all the while performing the internal calculus of when to abandon their original goal.

In a space battle distractions like that could easily be deadly, especially when one's opponent was an AI with faster-than-organic resources.

"Can I use the flamethrower?" Shinigami asked excitedly.

"We're in space, Shinigami." Barnabas studied the read-out. There were seven ships in the formation, all of them reading 'YCS' in their designation. 'Yennai Corporation Ship,' unless he was very much mistaken.

"I was thinking about that. If I vent a little bit of air next to the flamethrower—"

"No, we are not venting any of our air. This discussion is over."

"You are *so* boring. All right, hold on for a bit." The last words were broadcast to the whole ship as the *Shinigami's* jets rotated to send the ship tumbling end over end away from the enemy fleet.

Without any clear shot at a lock point for grappling hooks, the enemy ships waited—only to realize their mistake when the *Shinigami* stopped flipping and shot toward them at high speed.

"Wheeeee!"

"*Don't* ram them!"

"Don't worry, they'll move!" Shinigami pushed the engines and practically purred in satisfaction. She didn't exactly have what could be called sensations, but she had learned to interpret the flexing and vibrations within the ship in much the same way an organic life form would interpret feedback from their nervous system.

Right now, the ship "felt" damned amazing. It was flying at the limits of its capabilities for the first time in ages, and between the thrum of its engines and the dual challenges of evading the enemy fleet and keeping Barnabas and Gar safe Shinigami was thinking that today was shaping up to be a *very* nice day.

Plus, she got to shoot things.

She launched a spread of missiles. The other ship was playing chicken pretty well, holding its course as she barreled toward it, but as soon as the missiles began to close the captain clearly recognized that their options were limited. The ship dove under the *Shinigami,* only to expose itself to the guns on the undersides of her wings. Three sections of the hull breached and began to vent before the internal airlock doors closed, and the ship spun out of control, unable to avoid one of the guided missiles that had locked onto it.

"*Boom,*" Shinigami reported. Three of the other missiles struck home and the enemy fleet began to reorganize hastily. "Everyone hold on. The grappling hooks mean this battle is about ninety-five percent maneuvering."

"How do you calculate that?" Barnabas murmured. He narrowed his eyes at the screen. "Shinigami, if you are able to get into the center of their fleet and have several of them lock on, you might be able to pull them out of formation and into a collision course."

"I *like* that idea! Everyone keep holding on!"

Gar's voice came over the speakers, sounding breathless. "You can assume that I, at least, have not stopped holding on since this began. Barnabas, is there anything I could be doing?"

"I'm afraid not." Barnabas knew how upsetting it was to be in the middle of an event like this with no control over how anything unfolded and he felt a pang of sympathy for Gar. "Actually, perhaps you could see if you can find any information on these ships. They're affiliated with the Yennai Corporation, but exact registration and provenance might give us an idea of who they're calling in to mess with us."

"Right. I'll do what I can." He sounded pleased to have a distraction. Then, as several thuds reverberated through the hull, he asked with a deathly calm, "What was that?"

"Grappling hooks," Shinigami reported. "Okay, ah...hmm."

"I dislike when people dissemble." Barnabas had a sense he knew what was coming, but he asked anyway. "Shinigami, what are you planning?"

"Let's just say it has a high probability of working."

"Let's say more."

"No time!"

"No *time? Shinigami!*"

Shinigami opened the engines full-bore and the ship shot above the fray. She released seven full spreads of missiles behind her as she left the plane of battle. Yanked to the ends of their grappling hooks and then freed as the hooks popped away, the Yennai ships swung too close to one another. They tried to avoid collisions, and although some failed and some succeeded, none had the time or maneuverability to get out of the way of Shinigami's missiles.

On the bridge, Barnabas watched as the ships blinked off the trackers one after another.

There was only silence, broken by the beeping of a final proximity tracker that hastily shut off.

"What was that?"

"A ship appeared on the radar but then disappeared," Shinigami told him. "I'm scanning, but nothing is showing up now."

Barnabas swore softly. "What do you want to bet they had a ship waiting in the wings and now it's running home to tell them what it saw?"

"I should be able to see it, if so." Shinigami gave a low growl of frustration and brought up the outside view on the screens. "Do either of you see anything you shouldn't? It could just be designed to avoid scanning metrics and they're hoping we won't have eyes on it."

"I don't see anything," Barnabas told her a moment later.

"Me either," Gar reported. "Barnabas, is that supposed to be 'either' or 'neither?'"

"Either, I believe. I mean, either works. I mean, both terms could be used. You know, I really preferred Latin for ease of communication."

"The ship sailed on that one, man," Shinigami reported. "You need to let it go."

"Mmm. *Et Yennaiam delenda est.*"

"What?"

"*Ceterum censeo Yennai esse delendam.* Before the Third Punic War, Cato the Elder would end all of his speeches in the Roman Senate, no matter his topic, by reminding the other senators that Carthage must be destroyed. Until we have dealt with the Yennai Corporation, we will have a similar focus."

"I...see." Shinigami helpfully fed information from her data banks to Gar, who was presently trying to figure out the spellings of *any* of the words Barnabas had just used. "Well, then, what's our next move?"

"I'm thinking," Barnabas murmured. "Find us a rarely-traveled route and I'll get back to you."

In the rubble, hugging tight to a large piece of debris, Fedden's ship tumbled and spun out into space.

Tagurn's quick thinking had saved them again, hiding them in the natural movement of the debris field among other similarly-registered ships. Fedden had *seen* the *Shinigami* pause as it was flying away and knew it was looking for the hint of movement it would have seen on its tracking system.

It left, however, and Fedden stared at their own tracking system and struggled to breathe.

This was a nightmare. They had appeared too late, or so he had thought, and he'd had visions of his painful death playing behind his eyes until he saw the absolute destruction wreaked by the *Shinigami.*

Thank every god he'd ever heard of that they hadn't made it to the battle. If the captain of the *Get'ruz* had waited for them...

"We can't do this alone," Fedden declared finally. "We need more ships."

"And a trap," Tagurn agreed. "You can't take this ship on without stacking the deck, Fedden. And I think I have a plan."

14

"I ...*think*..." Gar pushed a piece forward on the chess board and grimaced. "Is that a legal move?"

"Not only is it a legal move, you're only four moves from—"

"*Shinigami.*" Barnabas glared.

"What? We're teaching him. It's a collaborative effort."

"You mean, I'm teaching him and you're hamstringing me."

"It's only fair. You know more about chess than he does. Theoretically. Your style of play disputes that, though. Yeah, I said that."

"I swear, when I find some way to punish AIs..." Barnabas made his move and closed his eyes. Between habit and his desire to win, it was taking great self-control *not* to scan Gar's mind—or whisper suggestions, much the same way he would speak to an Ubuara.

Would it work? Only experimentation could tell.

That would be unethical, he told himself.

Gar made the move Barnabas had been hoping for

anyway. It was a tempting move, sliding a bishop out to put Barnabas' king in check. However, it also allowed Barnabas to slide a rook down the center of the board and put Gar's king in checkmate.

Gar, to his credit, laughed as soon as Barnabas began to move the rook.

"I didn't look far enough ahead."

"It's easy to get caught up in the moment," Barnabas admitted. "Chess has been surprisingly...engaging."

Shinigami snickered. "He means infuriating, because he always loses."

"I do not *always* lose."

"More than fifty percent of the time."

"That is true, but only by a *very* small margin."

Gar, sensing that things might be getting dangerous, stood hastily. "I'm going to go, um...clean my room. Thank you for the game, Barnabas. I enjoyed it. I would be happy to play again sometime."

He swept out of the room before any chairs could be thrown and Barnabas smiled as the door hissed shut.

"He knows we're joking, surely?"

"Joking, shmoking. Most people don't think, 'eh, if I break a bone, I break a bone.' They try to avoid it, much like Gar tries to avoid you when you're about to start throwing chairs."

"How *do* these people pass the time, I wonder? Anyway, I only threw the chair that one time because you were launching books at me."

"A more sensible alternative would have been to use the chair as a shield."

"Mmm. I'll remember that for next time." Barnabas

went over to stare out of the window from the entertainment room.

"Another game?" Shinigami reset the board hopefully. She had a new strategy she'd been dying to test.

She had to admit that if it weren't for the organic element the game wouldn't have been any fun. She could analyze probabilities, but every so often Barnabas strung together a highly unlikely series of moves that seemed to occur to him out of nowhere. It kept Shinigami on her toes, as Bethany Anne would have said.

She would never have told him she just liked the game, however. That was the sort of thing he would take as a compliment, and he already had a big head.

He was so lost in thought right now that she had to repeat her question, and he shook himself as he looked at the speakers.

"I apologize, I was woolgathering. Not just now, I don't think. We need to figure out where we're going. I notice you've been taking us in the direction of the last known port of the *Get'ruz*." Shinigami and Gar had provided a detailed report of the shipping corporation's fleet.

"Yes. Would you like me to take us there faster?"

"I had something else in mind." Barnabas settled into one of the chairs by the window and smiled when Shinigami projected her avatar in one of the chairs opposite. "You're getting better at that."

The figure shrugged. Her arm lay along the back of the chair and one knee was crossed over the other. As Barnabas watched, she brushed her hair back over her shoulders.

"I hadn't realized how often humans made useless

movements," Shinigami remarked after showing off each of her recent additions. "None of you can sit *still*. Some of you are better at it than others, of course. *You're* pretty good at it, actually. But all of you are in motion most of the time."

"Such are the perils of having a central nervous system." Barnabas smiled. "And I had an idea about our next destination. It will be somewhat like finding a needle in a haystack, of course…"

"I'm intrigued."

"Ah, and here I was thinking you would finish my sentence. We caught the tail end of two communications when they went into formation to attack us. One was broad-wave, and they followed it up with what was clearly a conversation. But the other was sent in a specific direction where, as far as I can tell, there is nothing."

"You're thinking a secret base?"

"Possibly. Or maybe a communications hub." Barnabas smiled. "What do you want to bet Yennai Corporation has its own buoys to send and boost signals? And with our hook into Crallus' communications, we have at least an educated guess of where we might find one of those."

"So when you said a needle in a haystack, you really *meant* it." Shinigami pursed the avatar's lips and gave a low whistle. "You knew I couldn't resist the challenge. All right, course plotted and verified, and I'm adjusting our trajectory. Could any of your mindless ships back in the day do *that*, Grandpa?"

"When you call me that, it just motivates me to find out what your equivalent is of going to bed without supper."

"I take it you don't have fond memories of your grandparents?"

"I didn't talk back to them," Barnabas told her, unperturbed. "First because I was a child, then because I thought I was possessed by a demon, and—after that—because I had lost my mind." He frowned. "I don't know why people find pleasure in rehashing their old memories."

"Surely there are *some* pleasant ones." But Shinigami sensed this conversational topic might veer toward the thoughts that had saddened Barnabas in recent days. "Regardless, what are your plans when we *do* find the buoy? Because we will, I promise you that."

"I never had any doubts." Barnabas smiled. "It will be a long game, Shinigami. If we are going to do this without backup—and, as much as possible, I would like to—then we will need to be very, very careful. We cannot make the same mistake Gar just made in that chess game."

"Between the two of us, I doubt we will."

"Shouldn't it be the three of us?" Barnabas frowned contemplatively. "He should be more involved. His thought patterns have been well within acceptable ranges for a while and I can hardly expect him to develop better modes of behavior if I never give him any chances to *do* anything. Speaking of which, do you have recommendations yet on upgrades?"

"Fairly standard," Shinigami reported. She projected a scan of Gar's body on one of the smooth walls of the room. "The bones need to be strengthened, of course, and we'll want some changes to the cardiovascular structure to accommodate more movement. We won't know about the rest of the upgrades until he's moving more regularly and encountering impact."

"Which means we'll need to persuade him to do so."

"That shouldn't be hard. Tabitha left a whole series of kung fu movies in the data banks and he's been watching them religiously." Shinigami snickered. "He practices, too. He's actually got very fast reflexes."

"We are not teaching him kung fu."

"Too late, the damage is done."

"Right." Barnabas stood, shaking his head. "Well, we'll see to that once we know how soon we can expect to be involved in any altercations. For the next few weeks—or possibly months or even years—I think we can expect to be tracking down various parts of the Yennai Corporation, isolating them, and destroying them."

"How do you intend to keep the main piece of it from coming after you?"

"We'll learn their communication patterns and keep the communications going so that no one notices anything's amiss. If we can find a way to make it seem that they're still sending in a cut of profits while actually taking money, so much the better."

"Sneaky. I *like* it. Well, course laid in. I'll let you know when we're close."

Gar balanced on one leg, wobbling slightly. He had taken to chewing one lip when he was concentrating. It was a very human mannerism. He had never seen any other Luvendi do such a thing. It was surprisingly habit-forming, however.

On the holoscreen, the black-clad figure extended their leg, foot at the same height as their face, and then hopped several times to change feet. The flurry of potential strikes seemed to be designed to keep the opponent from getting within range.

Gar tried as hard as he could to get his foot up high, but the muscles in the backs of his legs simply wouldn't extend that far. He wound up with the leg bent, one knee against his thin chest, his foot straining to mimic the position of the human foot. This was agony.

Now the flurry of kicks. The other foot up, then the first, then the other, then the first again. One, two—

Gar came to looking at the ceiling dazedly. The pain was still fading from his body.

"What the…" He barely managed the words.

"I believe you forgot to plan how you were going to put your foot down," Shinigami answered. She sounded vaguely like she was struggling not to laugh.

"Have you been watching me?"

"Of course I've been watching you. I watch everything. Mostly. That, and I was worried you might get hurt. Don't worry, I scanned you while you were out. You didn't fracture anything."

"Uh-huh." Gar stared at the ceiling and decided that lying here seemed like a better idea than getting up. The floor wasn't *very* comfortable, but he was pretty sure it beat trying to move any part of his body.

"Come on, get up." Shinigami sounded impatient. "I wanna try something."

"Make your *own* body," Gar complained muzzily.

"I am heavily discouraged from doing so. It's one of the suggestions tagged 'Skynet.'"

"Huh?"

"Get uuuuuup."

Gar rolled over and draped his sleeves over his eyes. "You can't make me."

"No, but if I ever get to tweak your body and make you stronger, you'll still have to sit around here until you learn how to fight. Why not start now?"

Gar perked up; this sounded promising. "You think I could actually fight with Barnabas?" His practices so far had just been him daydreaming that he was the hero in these movies. They all fought for Justice and Honor, striking off on their own against impossible odds.

And in his opinion, they looked very dashing in their headbands. He was thinking he might start wearing one.

"Let's just say you need some practice," Shinigami offered diplomatically. "But yes, of course you could fight with Barnabas one day. We just need to make you less breakable."

"I am not a vase. Shinigami?" The AI had gone into gales of laughter.

"Just picturing you with a bunch of flowers stuck in your head. Never mind. Okay, so get back in the pose you were in before. One leg up. Yes, that's right. Now listen closely…"

15

The *Shinigami* floated in the blackness, cloaked and running as close to silently as it could. There was no way to determine what the communications buoy alongside them could detect.

Barnabas had honestly expected something very compact, more a signal collector and booster than anything else, but the "buoy" was instead a roughly cube-shaped cobbled-together collection of machinery about five meters to a side. It reflected the light of the stars very faintly.

Thankfully, it did not seem to be armed.

"I hate wearing space suits," Barnabas muttered. He checked the tether holding him to the ship and pushed himself off very slowly to cross the dozen or so yards between the ship and the buoy.

"It's no bulkier than a regular suit." Shinigami's tone said that he was being a baby about this.

"On the fingers, it is. I hate gloves. I was happy when gentlemen stopped wearing them. That was a long few decades." Barnabas caught the buoy and grimaced as it slowly began to turn. The last thing he needed while trying to assess strange electronics was to get dizzy.

"Why did you wear them if you hated them?"

"To be polite. Not liking an article of clothing was not a good enough reason not to wear it."

"You should have come up with a different fashion. That's how Scottish men got away with wearing no pants."

"Did Tabitha tell you that? Because I don't think you should be taking history lessons from her."

"No, that was Bethany Anne."

"Huh." Barnabas set a crawler loose on the surface of the buoy and watched as it began moving around.

They had modified the machinery to have limited gravitic fields in its tiny feet. Barnabas had originally suggested magnets, but Shinigami had pointed out that many electronics were sensitive to magnetic fields.

Barnabas crawled over the surface of the buoy, following the crawler until it disappeared abruptly into the innards of the machine. He followed it and peered down into the darkness, then switched on his flashlight.

"What are you hoping to see? You know you don't actually have the capabilities to watch the programming change, right?"

"I know that," Barnabas grumped.

"So?"

"So humans generally want to see things, even if it's a useless urge."

"Fair enough. I run statistical analyses even when the outcomes don't matter. We all have our quirks."

"I've started humming," Gar chimed in. "I don't know why."

"What *I* don't get is how you have such good pitch," Shinigami complained. "You said Luvendi don't make music and you don't care about music. And you really don't; I've scanned you for a physiological reaction. Humans have one, you don't. But your pitch and your timing are both spot-on."

"Is that why I've had 'Ode to Joy' stuck in my head for the past three days?" Barnabas asked suddenly. He looked over his shoulder at the ship. "Gar, are you doing a review of the classics?"

"If that is what Tabitha labeled as 'boring old-person music,' then yes."

Barnabas frowned. "I'm confused as to why she labeled it in the first place."

"She quite likes classical music," Shinigami revealed, and a moment later she added, "I've just remembered that she specifically asked me not to tell anyone that."

"Any other favorites?" Barnabas asked curiously.

"I've already said too much. I know nothing. You didn't hear any of it from me. Also, we have an uplink."

"Finally." Barnabas held out a hand and waited for the crawler to clamber out of the buoy and into his palm. "Shinigami, reel us in and open the Pod bay doors."

"I'm sorry, Dave. I'm afraid I can't do that."

"My name's not Dave."

"That's from *2001: A Space Odyssey*," Gar told him helpfully. "When the AI tries to kill the humans because they've abandoned the mission."

"How comforting. Shinigami, are you planning my death?"

"Not at all. Tabitha was also on a classic science fiction kick, so I watched some movies with her. Just don't abandon the mission and we should all be fine."

"How comforting. Well, open the Pod bay doors. I need to get these gloves off before I go insane."

Rald had spent enough time in the universe to know that bribes generally turned up more leads than beating the teeth out of possible informants until one of them started talking. It was unfortunate, but it was just how life was so he had come to terms with it.

It helped that he could go back to his preferred methodology once he had suspects.

In this case, he had run into a distressingly common roadblock: thwarted in their desire to own Devon's mines —he refused to use the new name of this planet—the Luvendi and the mercenaries had withdrawn to sulk and try to find other markets. None of them knew the names of the relevant humans. None of them had the information he needed.

So Rald had quietly made it known that he would pay for that information, and it was only a day and a half before a Nekubi slithered into his boarding house with some whispered names.

Which was why Rald was presently staring at the bruised and bloodied form of a Brakalon named Heddo-ran. He was the former guard captain at Venfirdri Lan's mines, the Nekubi had told him. He still worked there, for the mine workers. By choice. There were whispers that he had betrayed Lan, which had led to his death. Rald had snatched him while he was in Tethra to retrieve a shipment of supplies.

Having seen what was left of Jutkelon's compound, Rald didn't think the guard captain's defection was really to blame for Lan's death. It was clear that the humans would have triumphed with or without one Brakalon.

But Heddoran knew names, and Rald needed them. He paced in a slow circle around the Brakalon.

"So you don't know any humans."

"None." The Brakalon had, so far, barely seemed to notice that Rald was torturing him. Every once in a while he grunted as claws or a whip or a boot made contact, but the sound seemed more contemplative than anything.

Rald wasn't fooled. Heddoran was now bleeding heavily. Whatever self-control he had, it was close to breaking.

"Then you likely wouldn't mind if any humans were killed."

The Brakalon looked at Rald with a genuine smile now touching his swollen eyes. "No, but *you* will, if you're the one killing them."

Rald paused, his eyes narrowing.

"Word is, you want the humans who made all the changes on this planet." The Brakalon grinned, displaying the blood on his teeth. "They're more powerful than you can imagine. If you decide to hurt their kind you will find out what true pain is—and *then* it won't matter. You will be dead."

"True pain?" Rald grabbed a walking stick from the wall

and swung it as hard as he could into the Brakalon's torso. He heard ribs crack and the Brakalon gasped involuntarily. "Ah, so we *are* getting somewhere. Want another hit?"

"Hit me as much as you want." The Brakalon managed to get the words out, but his breath was coming in jerks now. "It won't make me know things."

"Yes, but you see, you *do* know things. Despite all your lies, you *do* know names. You were there, Heddoran. So let's start again." Rald swung the stick directly into the broken ribs again and the Brakalon gave an agonized yell. "There was a human at the mines. Was that the man who runs Aebura's?"

"No." The Brakalon sagged against the ropes. His head was lolling. "No."

"How can I believe you when you've lied so much? Maybe I should kill him just to be sure. Him and his mate —Elisa, is that her name? And the two brats. Little humans. I should wipe his line out down to the last drop of blood."

The Brakalon stared at him open-mouthed for a second. "It was a *kalanon*!"

"Oh?" Rald crouched to peer into his eyes. "Go on."

"It wasn't them. They're not… They just came here at the same time. The one at the mines was a *kalanon*. A priest."

Rald felt a stab of surprise. The priests he had met on his travels seemed uniformly useless, given to platitudes and philosophy. How could a priest take down an enterprise with so many guards?

"He's not there anymore." Now that Heddoran had started talking he couldn't seem to stop. "He left soon after. He's gone now, and he hasn't been back."

"What was his name?" When Heddoran didn't answer, Rald readied the stick again. "His *name*, Heddoran."

"Barnabas!" The Brakalon closed his eyes in defeat. "His name was Barnabas. Lan's second-in-command, Venfaldri Gar—he helped. He's with Barnabas now."

Finally, he had names—and an accomplice. The information brokers at Yennai Corp had thought Gar was dead. Rald smiled. "Really, there's only one last thing to ask. *Where is the mine?*"

Heddoran didn't answer right away, but Rald could see the hopelessness on his face. There was no way he could pretend not to know *that*. He had worked there for years. And while he had told himself he wouldn't say anything under torture, he had already begun to talk. He knew it was only a matter of time until he broke.

Rald thought the least he could do was help him make the decision to tell now rather than later. He let loose with the stick, raining blows on the bruised captive while the Brakalon screamed in pain. When the blows finally stopped, Rald was heaving for breath and smiling broadly. It had been a frustrating few days. He had needed this.

"I can do this again and again," he promised Heddoran. "But can you take that? It'll get worse as the bruises spread."

The Brakalon was barely conscious anymore. His lips moved, barely a whisper emerging. Rald leaned close and the Brakalon repeated himself, giving Rald coordinates and directions.

"Good," Rald soothed. He went to the door. "In return for the information you've given me, I'll give something back. If you survive these wounds, I won't kill you."

He left then, smiling in the early morning sunshine. He would collect a volunteer force from the mercenaries in town and they would be on the road by midafternoon. As for Heddoran... Well, there was no need to worry. He was too badly hurt to get himself out of the ropes, and even then it would take a miracle to cure him.

The noise of Tethra's market was loud enough, however, that Rald did not hear the door of the old warehouse creak open or see a figure steal inside.

Carter had been trailing Rald for two days now. The Ubuara had done everything they promised; they had been quick to alert him to where Rald was, and they tried to find out who he was talking to.

But Carter couldn't leave it up to them. He'd had a bad feeling about this since he'd heard about Rald talking to Elisa. He didn't like having Shrillexians around. He didn't like the fact that this one had gotten on-planet at all. The matter of the Luvendi and mercenaries was something Carter knew had been debated—should they be kept on-planet or allowed off, where they might spread the word of where High Tortuga was?

No one had come to any firm conclusions yet, but Carter *knew* they weren't supposed to be getting allies.

He'd been unloading crates of fruit at the bar this morning when one of the Ubuara came at a dead run to tell him Rald had taken Heddoran prisoner. Carter had grabbed his gun and his knife and gone as quickly as he could. Heddoran had a lot of things to atone for, after all, but he *was* atoning for them. He'd helped the Ubuara rebuild the mining town and he was keeping them safe. He was always pleasant when he stopped in at the bar, too.

And now he was in trouble.

Carter had arrived just in time to hear Heddoran give the Shrillexian Barnabas' name—to save Carter, Elisa, and the children.

Carter couldn't let him die now. He and the Ubuara began to undo the ropes that held Heddoran up and they eased him down as gently as they could.

"We're going to get you out of here," Carter promised Heddoran. "We'll get you a doctor. I promise."

"No...time." Heddoran grimaced. "You have to stop him. He's going to destroy the mine."

16

Crallus made his way out of the mess hall and up the sloping corridors toward his office. His steps were slow. He knew it was useless to avoid going back, but he did not want to. Since the Torcellan had come, Crallus spent his days doing more work than he had ever wanted to do—and the Torcellan treated him like a servant, to boot.

Crallus had taken over the syndicate because he didn't *want* to be treated like a servant. He was a damned mercenary. He took what jobs he wanted *when* he wanted. He hadn't liked listening to his first captain, so he had killed him and taken over the ship.

That had worked pretty well, so when old Goff had started to get a bit crazy, Crallus had figured it would work pretty well again.

It had—until now.

Until a few weeks ago, he'd been living the good life. He had a few fights now and again and ran missions occasionally, but mostly he just sat back and let the profits roll in.

He didn't worry much about the Yennai Corporation, because they didn't ask much. He passed along a share of the profits and any interesting news his ships' captains mentioned. As far as he could tell, Yennai had ignored that last part.

And then they didn't. Then he had a flurry of communications about the three ships that had answered a call for assistance and been summarily destroyed. Where had it been; where *exactly*?

Just when he had thought he was in the clear the Torcellan had shown up. He was vain, making sure his hair hung just so…and then putting that blasted hood over it.

Crallus supposed that was better than being expected to *ooh* and *aah* over his hair all the time. He had the suspicion that the Torcellan was that kind of male, wanting adoration for every little thing he did.

He'd set up shop in Crallus' office, though, and he seemed to expect Crallus to be *doing* things all the time.

What was there to do? Take some profits, keep an eye on the ships' captains to make sure they weren't getting uppity. It didn't take much to keep the syndicate running.

Crallus pushed the door open and nodded curtly to the Torcellan, who was sitting at Crallus' desk. "Good morning."

"It is not," the Torcellan replied in that soft-but-threatening way of his, "a good morning."

Crallus grunted and took a seat on the wide chair at the back of the room. There was nowhere else to sit, with that bastard in his desk chair.

The Torcellan swung around. "That ship has taken out more of ours, and we've confirmed it's the *Shinigami* under the control of a man named Barnabas. Ranger One."

"They sent video back?" Crallus asked interestedly.

"No. Our contact on Devon sent the information. Apparently, it's been difficult to find anyone who will talk. He's making headway, however, and is set to make...shall we say, an *example*."

"Of who?"

"Of the miners Barnabas 'liberated.'" The Torcellan said the word with deep disgust. "I hate revolutionaries. They're nothing but anarchists, deep down. They don't care if the world burns."

"Neither do you," Crallus retorted, finally unable to conceal his dislike. "You just like the money you get from how things are now."

There was a pregnant silence. "Careful," the Torcellan cautioned him finally. His voice was mild, but it sent chills along Crallus' spine. "I think you'll find that you don't want to offend us, mercenary."

Crallus lifted one shoulder and gave his best surly smile. A mercenary never showed fear. They knew how dangerous it was to behave like prey.

"So, this human took out *how* many more ships?"

The Torcellan looked at the computer screens, annoyed. "Seven, all registered to Get'ruz Shipping."

"I thought Get'ruz was a pirate group."

The Torcellan shrugged elegantly. "They owned ships and sold cargo."

A mercenary didn't bother with careful definitions. They called a gun a gun and a pirate a pirate. Crallus didn't care enough about the definitions to fight, however. He shrugged as well, ignoring the twinge of pain from his shoulder. "If they didn't send the video—"

"They had several ships coming along the same route, and apparently some of the wreckage was identifiable. Seven ships destroyed, and for all we know they didn't even manage to land a shot on the *Shinigami.*"

"There's no way to know it even *was* the *Shinigami.*"

"It was," the Torcellan stated darkly. "Who else would have destroyed seven ships and not even have mentioned it? If it were a business rival there would be gossip right now. There is none. We've checked."

Crallus considered the Torcellan's point. That, at least, made sense.

"Get'ruz's ships were registered to us," the Torcellan informed him pointedly. "If they noticed that, they know who we are."

"Which means they're coming for us," Crallus finished. He accepted with reticence that his syndicate was part of the Yennai Corporation. It didn't seem very fair that he'd sent in those profits for years and now he was being asked to go up against the corporation's enemies, but that was just how things shook out when you weren't in power.

Maybe he'd kill whoever was in charge of the Yennai Corporation and move up. It had worked twice now, so it might work again.

"Yes," the Torcellan agreed. "We've seen how the humans respond to such things. Once provoked and attacked, they come after anything and everything their enemies own. We must be ready. They will either come for the central Yennai base as soon as they find out where it is, or yours. I have already ordered both to be placed on high alert, and we should withdraw there as soon as possible. I'm having both of them stocked with food and ammunition as well."

Crallus sighed. "I'll go tell the captains to leave this base. It can be cleared by tomorrow morning."

"Give them six hours," the Torcellan advised. "No more. Once they come for you, humans do not hesitate. That base is one of the few secure places they can go. If the humans catch them here or on one of their ships they're as good as dead."

"I'll call Fedden back in, then."

"No." The Torcellan had stood and now he looked at Crallus, and the Brakalon had the sense of narrowed eyes. "Fedden must earn his way back into the syndicate or die trying."

"He *will* die trying! If seven ships couldn't take on the *Shinigami*, how is he supposed to—" Crallus broke off as he understood. "You never believed he'd survive it."

"Of course not." The Torcellan brushed a speck of dirt off his sleeve. "But allowing someone to earn redemption and have them fail is much less unpopular with the sort of people you employ. It was the only smart thing to do."

Do you not care about anyone? Crallus grimaced and held his tongue rather than spit those words out.

He knew the answer anyway.

"They're mobilizing forces," Shinigami reported later that evening.

"Oh?" Barnabas looked up from the table, which was

strewn with documents and the remains of dinner. He and Gar had been poring over lists of companies affiliated with the Yennai Corporation, and the documents were now covered in Barnabas' handwritten notes. He'd rolled his sleeves up to work and he ran a hand through his already-disheveled hair as he waited for more information.

"They've given the order for about half their various guards to come to the Yennai HQ, which I have no idea how to find. The other half is supposed to form a unified fleet, I'm guessing to search for us, and Crallus has issued orders to his ships to go to their fortified base. They're leaving soon. I'd say they'll probably be backup for the fleet if necessary."

"Ah." Barnabas chuckled with great satisfaction. "Well, that's just...convenient."

"What is?" Gar frowned. "I've seen what this ship can do, but those bases are *heavily* fortified. It will be difficult to infiltrate them."

"We don't have to." Barnabas was smiling now. "And indeed, we shouldn't. A few centuries back—well, more than that, now—humanity would lay siege to cities. It would have been quite effective but for the fact that the army also required large amounts of supplies. The lesson, in short, is not to besiege cities. In this case, however... they're going into seclusion on their own."

"So?" Gar looked confused.

"He means we'll just wait them out," Shinigami interjected. She sounded pleased. "Bomb off, do something unrelated."

"Bomb what?"

"She's saying we would leave," Barnabas explained.

"Given her near-constant mentions of bombs being used for their intended purpose, I can see how you would be confused."

"It's not that. It's the fact that your language is insane." Gar crossed his arms. "I keep trying to learn things, and then you use words in ways that make no sense."

"Mmm. In any case, she's quite right. I propose we let these people hide away in their bunkers. We have all the time in the world, after all. We can let them drain their resources and begin to get complacent and go stir-crazy while *we* go after the parts of the corporation they didn't bring with them. When they finally emerge and give us an opening, they'll find that most of their corporation is gone —and in the meantime, they will have gotten rusty."

"So they're…they're afraid of you coming to kill them, so they're hiding away and you're just going off to kill other people?" Gar reminded himself how little he wanted to get on Barnabas' bad side.

"Precisely," Barnabas agreed.

"And I'm guessing from his tone that he already has someone in mind," Shinigami added.

"I do indeed. If you would bring up the files on the Boreir Group, please?"

"Ah, him again. He was involved in munitions, wasn't he?" Shinigami whistled as she brought up the file. "*Damn, he really is. You don't think small, do you?*"

The Boreir Group was presently owned by a third-generation employee named Mustafee Boreir, a Yofu male. The company provided munitions to several governments and major mercenary groups. Their production facilities, which were scattered across several sub-corporations, made them one of the largest munitions manufacturers in known space.

"They haven't been sent after us and they haven't been called to the base," Barnabas informed them. "But I'm betting that if push comes to shove, Yennai is going to want more munitions to throw at us. I suggest we wait until we have confirmation that Yennai's head honchos are in the last steps of their retreat to the stronghold. In the confusion, we attack the headquarters of the Boreir Group, and Shinigami takes up communications so that Yennai is unaware anything has gone wrong. From there we dismantle the whole damned thing. Over the course of the next few months, we shut down all of their facilities and sell them and offload any cargo ships they owned and any remaining inventory—as much as possible to the Federation—thus cutting off one of the most profitable and dangerous parts of Yennai's holdings."

Gar nodded. "At a few months per group, though, we'll be here for quite a while."

"We won't need to have much active involvement day to day," Barnabas explained. "Shinigami can handle most of it once the stronghold is secure without even taxing her processing powers. Isn't that right, Shinigami?"

"Quite correct. I'll also be diverting Yennai's incoming payments into untraceable accounts. When they finally come out of their hidey-hole, they won't have any money left."

"Destroy them from the ground up," Barnabas agreed. "I like it."

"You want something else to like? I think I have an idea to get you into the headquarters…"

17

Two days later Rald headed out of Tethra on his way to the mines. He took no one with him, just a battered old vehicle and some supplies.

He wasn't fool enough to risk all the forces he might call on just yet, but he *had* left instructions behind. Many of the miners, it turned out, had come to Tethra after their contracts were up, and they had built lives here. They were rebuilding the mine as their own now, so they had left their families and businesses unprotected.

Idiots. Rald smiled coldly. Did they not think anyone would figure out what they had done here? Did they not think they had put targets on themselves?

They were going to be too dead to learn their lesson, but others would see it.

As for the humans everyone was so afraid of...let them come over here if they cared. It was clear that this continent wasn't their priority. They had freed the mines and then gone off somewhere else.

Rald was betting that they weren't going to come back.

He'd heard some stories of big battles on the other side of the planet. The humans were all occupied. They weren't going to bother themselves with this, and by the time they did, their forces would be battle-weary and the people who *really* owned Devon would be strong again.

After all, he had the backing of the Yennai corporation now, didn't he?

He thought he heard the distinctive chitter of one of the rodent-creatures nearby—what had the guards called them, 'Ubuara?'—but when he turned to look he saw nothing. They seemed to make a point to stay out of his way, though he saw them everywhere.

Good. They knew he wasn't to be trifled with.

The wheels of the truck squelched through the mud and Rald took a look over his shoulder at the weapons he had been able to buy in Tethra. He growled softly in disappointment. He preferred his own weapons, but even Yennai Corporation's contacts hadn't been enough to get those on-planet.

He could make do.

He thought of Jutkelon as he drove. The Brakalon had been a stubborn old bastard, not much like the other Brakalons Rald had known. They tended not to run their own companies, just take posts on other people's ships— like a lot of Shrillexians.

Maybe that was why Rald and Jutkelon had gotten along so well. Neither of them had been sure that they wanted to run their own outfits; they just didn't want to have to answer to rich assholes anymore. Jutkelon had eventually gone back to being part of a bigger group, but for a few years they had worked well together.

You couldn't go through that many firefights with someone, escape that many close calls, have them save your back and you save theirs so many times, *without* there being an obligation. Other mercenaries—the ones Rald had fought with once or twice—he wouldn't do this for them. However, he had spent too long fighting at Jutkelon's side to let him be killed like this and not avenge his death.

They'd wanted to make a point, the bastards. They'd left that smoking crater at Jutkelon's compound so no one would want to stand up to them anymore.

Rald's growl got louder and he narrowed his eyes.

The first step was finding out what was in this mining town. Once he knew what was there, he would call in reinforcements and wipe it off the map.

Fedden ducked under a low doorway and gave it an annoyed look.

This space station had been made for some race smaller than Shrillexians, not to mention it was practically falling apart, it was so old. Hopefully there were some larger corridors somewhere, or Namkelon was going to have to crawl to get around.

That mental image, at least, was funny enough to make Fedden bare his teeth in a grin.

"You ready?" Tagurn asked from behind him.

Both Shrillexians ducked through another door. They could hear the clamor of voices from ahead. Fedden had called everyone he could think of to this meeting and he'd told Namkelon to do the same. The Brakalon was cautious by nature, so Fedden was sure he'd only choose people who could be trusted.

Besides, with Crallus retreating, what was he going to do if the ships' captains started to do their own thing?

Nothing; that was plain.

Fedden wasn't a fool. He'd seen the wreckage of the Get'ruz fleet. He'd put two and two together easily when Crallus and his mysterious Torcellan friend had withdrawn to the main base that Crallus had never used before now.

They were afraid of these humans. Clearly, they had sent Fedden to die.

He had no intention of doing that.

He came around a bend in the corridor and a guard at the main door nodded at them. Fedden recognized him as Namkelon's first mate. So the Brakalon was cautious enough to have guards posted, then. The alien swung the big airlocked door into the main room wide, and as it opened the noise inside blasted into the corridor.

Fedden had seen how many ships were outside, but he was still impressed to see how crowded the space was.

They fell silent as he entered, and he noticed that they didn't seem so much happy to see him as discontented with the way things were.

He could work with that. He made a show of greeting Namkelon and exchanging a few words with him, as well as nodding to a few of the other captains he knew well.

"You've gathered a large crowd," he told Namkelon appreciatively.

"It wasn't a hard choice," Namkelon told him bluntly. "Get shut up like prey in a cage with that Torcellan, making no contracts, or stay out here? No one wanted to retreat except Crallus. And his favorites, of course."

Fedden sighed. He had hoped that one or two of Crallus' favorites might join them. Their ships were state of the art. It paid to be in Crallus' good graces, but he'd chosen his inner circle long ago and it took too much ass-kissing to work your way in at this point.

Ah, well. They'd do this with or without him and his best ships. They had numbers on their side now.

And if those numbers were only here because they didn't like Fedden's rival? Well, he could work with that.

"Thank you all for coming," Fedden called to the group that filled the room.

This main chamber had multiple levels with walkways around the edges of the main column, and those walkways were packed with mercenaries leaning down to watch him. He saw friends and rivals, new fighters and grizzled old ones.

They all had some of the same reasons, though.

"Things have really gone to shit, huh?" Fedden asked them.

There was a sudden burst of laughter and a few of the mercenaries nodded.

Fedden grinned up at them. "Crallus was never the best of us, but he didn't get in our way, right? We had a place to come back to, exchange information, get some bigger jobs. Crallus didn't take too much. It worked...but now he's getting weird."

No laughter now. The nods became serious. No one liked the way things had been going recently.

"When was the last time Crallus helped any of you get a

job?" Fedden asked. "I'm not talking those shit ones guarding cargo ships, twenty guards for a whole damned hauler and no way in hell of making your bonus. I mean the *good* jobs."

No one answered. Crallus *hadn't* helped them out recently.

"But when was the last time Crallus called you up to bitch about how you were doing, how much of a take you were sending through, or ask you to go do a favor for him?"

Mercenaries called out answers. For most, it had only been a few days. Crallus hadn't asked much before that, but he'd been insufferable for a while now. Everyone here was quick to see that this could easily become the new normal.

"Not to mention," Fedden added with a grin, "when was the last time you got back to base, had some food, and thought it might actually kill you?"

They were laughing again.

"And while he's always talked about raising rates," Fedden finished, "he's actually *going* to raise them this time. When he's asking more of us than he ever has and giving back less!"

Their faces were angry now, and he knew he'd successfully tapped their discontent.

Now came the sell, and he could only hope he'd done enough.

"You know why he's going back to his base, right?" Fedden looked at their expressions. They *didn't* know. Good. Offering new information was one of the best ways to get allies. "He's gotten the syndicate dragged into something bigger than he is. Him and his Torcellan? They've fucked up, and they were willing to throw us into the crossfire to fix it."

There was a sudden furious silence.

"That's right." Fedden walked in a slow circle, his voice rising. "You remember Crallus sending those ships off to Devon? Getting those people killed? Well, he tried to throw me at them too. Turns out he never thought I'd survive. He'd just get to execute me without having to do it himself."

"You shot him," someone called from the gallery above.

"Like you never wanted to!" Fedden yelled back and there was another burst of laughter. Some of the mercenaries pounded on the railings in approval. "I tried it, it didn't work. But I wonder—did he ever even ask if you wanted things to change? Did he ever even *ask* if there was something bigger behind the Torcellan's plans? No, he just told you all to abandon your contracts and sit in a cage waiting for someone to come shoot at you.

"He's pissed off someone bigger than you can imagine," Fedden continued. "You know why he's retreating? He sent those three ships and they got destroyed, so he and that Torcellan, they sent seven more ships. State of the art pirate ships. Get'ruz Shipping, not a small outfit. All *those* ships got destroyed too, and they were only trying to take on *one.*

"Well, now Crallus is running—him and the Torcellan. They want us to go with them so we can be security, just sitting there waiting. Does that sound like a good idea to anyone?"

Heads shook, and there were growls and a few derisive shouts.

"Doesn't sound good to me either," Fedden told them. "So here's my plan: we lay a trap for this one ship rather than waiting for them to learn about our base and kill us all. I can get a message to that ship to tell them the terms—they won't be able to resist coming to meet us. And when they're dust, we'll start a new syndicate. Half the fees of Crallus', none of the bullshit he's been pulling lately, and a hell of a lot more jobs when our clients hear who we managed to take out. Who's with me?"

Only a few hung back; the rest called out acceptances. Fedden pointed out their captains with easy familiarity and beckoned for them to come down to join him.

"Come on down and I'll lay out the plan. Let's get this show on the road."

"Okay, but are we *actually* sure this is going to work?" Gar paced around the bridge, throwing concerned glances at the viewscreen, where a ship was growing closer by the second.

"Of course not." Barnabas sat quite composedly in the captain's chair. "Nothing is ever *sure*. Take a seat, won't you?"

He was wearing hooded robes with the hood presently pushed back, and as to the rest of his disguise…

Well, Gar couldn't believe they were going to try to pull this off. From start to finish, the plan was insane.

"They haven't noticed us yet," Shinigami pointed out.

"How can you possibly know that?" Gar glared at one of the speakers and rubbed his face. It was another human mannerism he had picked up. "We're going to get blasted off the side of the ship like we're target practice. Which we will be. For an automated system, no less."

"Shinigami thinks it's unlikely they'll notice us," Barnabas soothed.

"Unlikely." Shinigami snorted. "No, I said they *won't*. Their security systems look for active ships without the Boreir Group security codes, and we won't *be* an active ship when they see us." There was a pause. "You *are* going to turn me back on, aren't you?"

"That depends on whether you intend to keep making insane plans," Gar shot back.

Barnabas chuckled.

"Laugh it up, blondie," Shinigami muttered. She flickered into existence as a projection.

Barnabas shut up and glared at the projection as it took a seat. "It's a *wig.*"

"It's blond. Also, you look ridiculous."

"I *look* like a Torcellan."

"Only if nobody looks too hard," Gar muttered. "I just want to ask again, are we *sure* this is going to work? Because this. Is. Insane."

"None of it is insane; every part of it is logical. I'm an AI, so I literally *can't* be insane. I *only* make good plans."

"I was with you right up until that last part," Barnabas told her. "May I remind you that you once suggested using guided missiles during an interrogation?" *Also,* he added silently, *let's not tell Gar that was his interrogation, shall we?*

Good call. "That was entirely logical. First, I didn't think you were going to get anything more out of them, so we didn't need it to be an interrogation anymore. Second, I wanted to use them, so it was only logical to do so. Third, unrelated to the missiles but important, we're almost ready to dock. You should get to the airlock."

"Indeed." Barnabas' lips twitched. He stood and flipped the hood over his face. The white-blond hair of the wig was just visible beyond the hood and the skin of his hands, made artificially paler, looked Torcellan if one only glanced at them. He nodded to Gar. "I leave the ship in your hands. I will communicate when it is time to turn it back on."

He left the bridge before Gar could again plead with him to call the plan off.

He had to admit it was an audacious plan; there was no doubt about that. Boreir Group controlled an entire planet and several moons, around which they had positioned a massive security system. The autonomous weapons systems that comprised it were attuned to spot engine emissions, heat, communications of any sort, electrical activity, and many more subtle indicators of approaching ships.

Any object giving off any of those signals and *not* broadcasting the correct security codes on the correct channels would be blown to smithereens.

They had thought about trying to evade the system, but a quick review of its capabilities and known kills showed that this would probably be far too time-consuming to pull off within the window they had. After all, they needed to do this while the Yennai Corporation bigwigs would probably not be on the lookout for small flickers in their transmissions from the subsidiary groups.

And taking out the system—or even part of it—was the sort of thing that might attract too much attention.

The answer they came up with had been elegantly simple—attach themselves to a Boreir Group ship, power down, and use its signal to mask them and get them through the shield.

They had chosen their ship carefully. It was one of the smaller cargo haulers that had completed its delivery and was returning empty to pick up another load of munitions. Since it was not filled with valuable explosives and it wasn't one of their bigger ships, it wasn't presently being guarded by other ships whose crews might see the *Shinigami*.

You could fool electronics, but fooling the eyes was a lot more difficult.

That had been step one. Step two was getting Barnabas onto that ship to get the security codes for their use on the way out and wreak whatever havoc he could, before sneaking him back off, undocking, and flying away to land on the planet.

"Since we'll be there anyway…" he had explained to Gar.

Gar apparently did not agree. He'd been pleading with them for the past two days to reconsider.

Barnabas shook his head and smiled. Gar would learn. He was willing to bet that within six months Gar would be making plans that were just as audacious. He was already beginning to give as good as he got when they all traded insults.

Meanwhile, Shinigami was guiding the ship ever closer to the cargo hauler. They were still a ways out from the shield, so she could take her time. Her systems were in overdrive as she scrambled their signals and masked her emissions so that no one on the ship would notice them, and she had to align the ships carefully before docking so that the sound of it wouldn't reverberate through the hull.

It was difficult to guide two high-speed ships into

perfect alignment, but Shinigami had reflexes better than any human pilot. She had the two ships right next to one another before her airlock extended and coupled to the other ship's.

She scanned their frequencies and saw no alerts from any quarter. Whatever was happening inside the ship, no one seemed to have noticed their presence yet.

"You're good to go," she told Barnabas.

"Thank you." He stepped into the airlock and pushed himself down the corridor, briefly weightless. At the other end, he attached a small override module and allowed Shinigami to work her magic on the passcodes that held their side of the airlock door in place.

Shinigami scanned the hallway inside and waited until it was unoccupied before opening the door. Barnabas turned himself the right way up, stepped through, and closed the door behind him.

Going offline now, Shinigami told him.

Gar will turn you back on, Barnabas assured her. *And if he doesn't for some reason, I'll make sure to do it before I kick his ass so you get to watch.*

You're the best friend an AI could ask for.

I'll remind you of that.

He set off into the corridors with a smile. A few moments later he felt Shinigami's silent presence in his mind disappear, and Gar reported quietly in his earpiece.

"The ship is offline."

Thank you, Barnabas murmured back. They hadn't wanted to fit Gar with a communication chip just yet, but he had a receiver that could translate Barnabas' silent communication into speech for him. *We'll stay radio-silent from here on out unless something goes very wrong.*

"Understood."

Barnabas heard footsteps coming up the corridor toward him and he bowed his head, moving purposefully. He must keep his face hidden. If anyone looked closely it would be clear that he wasn't Torcellan.

"Hey, you. Captain says to—" The alien's voice broke off as she approached Barnabas. His eyes flicked up and he saw her examining him.

Damn. Shinigami, things are about to get—

He remembered that she was not there to talk to and stopped his monologue. A moment later, scanning the alien's mind, he realized that she was terrified.

"I didn't realize you were aboard," she apologized, bowing her head.

Barnabas came to a halt and simply looked at her. Whoever this alien believed he was she was treating him with deference, so he would act as though it was his due. When she looked up, he nodded slowly and followed her with his head as she edged around him and set off again. He could *feel* her trying not to break into a run.

Please let him not know who I am. When did he come on board? I have to tell the captain. He probably knows already…

Her thoughts, fractured and afraid, faded as she moved away and Barnabas frowned slightly.

This was a complication he hadn't anticipated. This crew member, and likely others, seemed to believe he was not only *a* Torcellan but a very specific one. What if one of them had specific questions?

He would need to take less time on this ship than he

had anticipated, and be more cautious. At the very least they were afraid of him, but who knew how far that would get him?

He made his way to one of the rooms that gathered communications and batched them out. The sheer volume of emitted communications on all frequencies made these places dangerous for most life forms while the communications were active—but Barnabas was not "most life forms." Gritting his teeth against the hum and the static charge in the air, he eased his way inside and shut the door behind him.

Step three was to hook into their communications so they could come and go at will. Who could say when they might need to come back, or what protocols they would need in order to land? Barnabas affixed another device and began to search through the ship's protocols.

To his delight, everything was organized very neatly within its data banks. The ship itself was programmed to respond to the queries passed along by the shield system, feeding the information broadcast by them to another algorithm in the ship.

Barnabas had not anticipated that the shield system would emit part of its own key, but that was genius. Very few people would think the solution might lie there, of all places. He found the algorithm and copied it, then studied the itinerary.

Shinigami had devised a protocol that would change the ship's destination and auto-steering but not prevent the captain from receiving any route change instructions sent over Boreir channels. The ship would return itself to the trajectory Barnabas wanted it on, even if the captain somehow figured out that they were going to the wrong place—but it was extremely unlikely that he would.

This ship would return to the black and deliver the munitions to the middle of nowhere, and as soon as it was far away it would dump the coordinates. Barnabas could figure out what to do with the munitions later.

He would have stayed, but the knowledge that the people on board were on the lookout for a particular Torcellan changed his mind. He hastened back toward the airlock, opened it, and climbed inside. Once across the little corridor he rapped on the *Shinigami's* door and waited for Gar to open it.

The Luvendi was frowning when the door swung inward. "Is something wrong? You're back sooner than I expected." He fell in beside Barnabas as they made their way back to the bridge. "About ten minutes until we pass through the shields, I think."

"Nothing's wrong, precisely." Barnabas pressed his lips together as he thought. "But they didn't just mistake me for a Torcellan, they mistook me for one they're afraid of. So somewhere out there, there's a Torcellan who goes around hooded like this. Someone who's high up in their organization."

"Or the Yennai Corporation."

"Or that. Good point." Barnabas took a seat in the captain's chair and considered that while the cargo ship passed through the shields. He noticed Gar radiating tenseness as they went through, but after a while it was clear that the shield had not noticed their presence.

"Let's turn the ship back on," Barnabas instructed. "And go catch us some munitions dealers."

Carter had been aware of Rald leaving Tethra within a few minutes of it happening. He had a hopper prepped, so it was quick work to find Oemuga and follow him.

"Be safe while I'm gone," he told Elisa seriously. "If you have so much as a hint that Rald has come back, you go hide with the Ubuara."

"I don't think I can fit inside any of their houses." Elisa laughed at his fussing. "The kids certainly could, though." She regretted saying that when Carter went pale. "Carter, we're going to be *fine*. For all we know, this Shrillexian's truck is going to sink into the swamp or something."

"He got the jump on Heddoran," Carter reminded her. "I don't like that. Look, maybe for the next few days—"

Elisa put a finger to his lips with a smile. "We'll be fine," she repeated. "Now *go*. The sooner you warn them, the sooner you can come back." She handed him a big bottle of Pepsi. "For the road."

"God, I love you." Carter grinned and kissed her. He

knelt for two very sticky kisses from the twins—they had clearly gotten into the *hakoj* pallets again—and headed off to the hopper.

To his surprise, Heddoran was already there. He took up most of the hopper and was glaring at anything and everything. Carter assumed this was the Brakalon's way of hiding his pain. He was frankly surprised that the former guard captain was even able to walk.

"I know," Heddoran grizzled when Carter opened his mouth. "But no one knows that camp better than I do. If you want to defend it you need to bring me…and I have to tell them it was me who gave away their location, too."

Carter took one look at the Brakalon's face and gave up his plan to talk him into another course of action. "Very well, then. Hold on."

He tried to pilot the hopper as gently as he could, but with the Brakalon on board it was a bumpy journey. And since Rald being on the roads necessitated that they fly the long way around to stay out of sight, it was a long journey as well. It was late afternoon before they arrived, and the mines were just letting out for the day when the hopper set down in the main square.

Someone must have recognized Heddoran before they even set down because Aebura was already in the square when they arrived. She bounded onto the railings of the hopper and launched into an impassioned monologue in her own language, with a lot of gesturing.

To Carter's surprise, Heddoran listened all the way through. He didn't speak Ubuara—no one really did except them—but he seemed to correctly interpret her words as dismay and not a little bit of scolding.

"I'm sorry," the Brakalon told them humbly. "I've failed you."

Aebura threw a look at Carter. "Carter Eastbourne, tell him that he has *not* failed us."

"I gave the location of the mine to someone who wants to hurt you," Heddoran blurted before Carter could answer. "I was afraid of what would happen if I did not. After I have helped you fight him off I will resign my post at once."

The crowd had gone quiet when he'd admitted what he had done and now they whispered amongst themselves as Aebura swayed side to side, deep in thought. A few of the Ubuara exchanged glances, clearly communicating mind-to-mind as Ubuara did.

"Start at the beginning," Aebura told him finally.

"Maybe we shouldn't discuss this here—" Carter began.

She only frowned in response and he realized a moment later how strange that must sound to an Ubuara. While other species would hide their leaders away so they wouldn't start a panic by discussing the imminent attack, the Ubuara would all know what was going on by sensing Aebura's thoughts.

"We *all* hear," Aebura told him firmly. "Heddoran, explain."

"His name is Rald," Heddoran began. "He's a Shrillexian. He used to fight with Jutkelon. Jutkelon even mentioned him once or twice. They were old friends. I don't know how he found out what happened, but he had a lot of questions. He threatened to hurt Carter's family if I didn't tell him the names of the people who killed Lan and Jutkelon—

and where the mine was. I should have kept my mouth shut and fought harder."

"It wasn't your fault," Carter argued fiercely.

"Carter Eastbourne is right." Despite Carter's many reminders, Aebura tended to use his full name. "There were many in the town who knew where the mine was. He would have found one of them if you hadn't given him the answers—and you would be dead."

Heddoran was glowering. He didn't seem to think this excused his behavior, but he clearly knew better than to argue with Aebura once she'd made up her mind. Carter sympathized. Although he'd known the Ubuara for only a few weeks he had already seen how stubborn she could be, and she always surprised him with her unique combination of forgiveness and fierce idealism.

"What do we do now?" she asked the two of them, looking back and forth.

"Fortify this place," Heddoran growled as he heaved himself up, going a bit grey as his cracked ribs shifted. He stomped toward the guard barracks. "Too much of it is flammable," he muttered. "Have to form fire brigades, but we'll need the water in case they try to wait us out…"

His voice grew fainter and Carter sighed as he looked after the Brakalon.

"I wish he hadn't insisted on coming. He should be resting."

"When people want to protect their home, it is rude to tell them to let other people handle it," Aebura suggested wisely. Her tail twitched. "Which is why I have not told you to go back to Tethra where it is safer and stay with your family."

"And leave all of you here undefended? Never." Carter held up an arm and smiled when she ran up it to perch on his shoulder. "Come on, we'd better follow him and see what he's up to."

It was evening when Rald finally got close to the mine. He had left the truck on the side of the road a few miles away and charted a path through the foothills so no one would see him approach.

Now he was crouching on one of the hills that overlooked the town and studying the place through binoculars. They weren't made for a Shrillexian, but they were enough for him to get an idea of what he was doing.

Several of the guards at the bar in Tethra had suggested that maybe the guard force at the mine had stayed on. Rald had thought they were being ridiculous, but apparently they had been correct. The guards seemed to have training, too. They weren't just miners taking shifts on the walls.

He was also pretty sure he had seen Heddoran. He swore at that. He should have just killed the Brakalon when he had the chance. He'd wanted the male to suffer, though, so he'd left him unattended.

He wouldn't make that mistake again.

He opened a channel to his contacts in Tethra.

"No big surprises here. Bring everyone out. *Everyone.*" He smiled. The miners liked to think they were so clever, sacrificing for each other.

Rald knew just how to break that spirit.

It wasn't very long before Fedden and his team settled on a place for the ambush.

Once he'd outlined his specifications, captains had started throwing out suggestions. Some places were too easily navigated in a spaceship, others didn't have enough cover. Many didn't have the unique lure Fedden had told them the place *must* have.

But eventually, Loriq had suggested a place that was perfect. As soon as she said the name, everyone had started nodding. A quick look at the specifications on the screen showed them that no one was misremembering.

It had all the qualities they needed.

"Do we send the message?" one of them asked eagerly.

It had been a bad few weeks. Everyone was ready for a fight. They might not like being cannon-fodder, but none of them wanted to let this human bastard get away with what he'd done either.

Fedden wanted nothing more than to throw out the challenge here and now, but he knew better than that.

"Not yet," he told them. It felt good to have people looking at him with respect and taking his orders. "First we get into position and *then* we send the message. I don't want any chance of this going wrong. That ship is fast."

They nodded at the wisdom of that and filed out. Only Tagurn remained behind.

"It's going well," Tagurn offered.

"It wouldn't be going at all without you." Fedden nodded to him. He planned to give Tagurn half his share from this job. He knew better than to take the male for granted, since that was how captains got killed in their sleep. He frowned. "Why haven't you tried to take over this whole thing for yourself?"

Tagurn shrugged. "I like the fighting, but I don't like the politics. You went out there shaking hands and smiling at people. You can do all that. Just give me plenty of enemies to fight and I'll be happy."

"Oh, you'll have no shortage of those," Fedden assured him. He smiled now. "When this part is over, you know we'll need to take that base from Crallus and his pet captains. And while you say you don't want a ship, well... one of those nice shiny ones will be there for you if you ever change your mind."

Tagurn smiled fiercely and clasped his hand. "Looking forward to the fight. The ship...eh. Maybe someday, but for now I fight with you. I knew you'd be here someday."

"There's a lot of people between us and our own syndicate," Fedden warned.

"That's what makes it a good plan. You need worthy opponents or it's no fun."

Fedden grinned. Tagurn's bloodthirsty humor was infectious. Worthy opponents, yes—they needed those or they would get soft. He was treating this mission with the respect it deserved. The *Shinigami* was a worthy opponent indeed.

But surely even *that* ship couldn't withstand this fleet.

2 0

With the passcode algorithms extracted from the cargo ship and the true identity of the *Shinigami* masked, they were able to set down quite easily. One of the series of domes below retracted to reveal a landing pad. The dome slid back into place as they touched down and the room was carefully re-pressurized before they disembarked. The deck crew ascertained that there was no cargo to unload and took no further notice of them.

Sloppy, Barnabas remarked to Shinigami. His lip curled, hidden under the hood he'd pulled up once more to disguise himself. *It's sloppy, and they should be ashamed of themselves.*

Knowing you, you're not going to give them much time to feel ashamed before they're dead. But the shield is incredibly good. We barely got around it.

So they should just assume that no one ever would? Barnabas shook his head. *Any system can be conned. The moment you put absolute trust in something like that you start the clock toward your execution.*

Not only that, it's boring. I mean, they could have given us a real challenge, but no.

Don't tempt fate. Barnabas paused at the door to the main compound and looked over his shoulder at the ship. *And remember the new rule: if someone tries to steal you,* tell *me.*

Yeah, yeah. I took care of it last time, if you remember.

By the skin of your teeth. Tell me anyway.

Fiiiiine.

Barnabas shook his head as he emerged into the corridor, but he was smiling.

He walked quickly. The landing pads were not close to the control center for the headquarters. It was a small concession to security, given that none of the personnel seemed to be instructed to request authorization or question visitors.

The Boreir Group's headquarters was on a rocky planet with an atmosphere that didn't appear to have ever nurtured life. Shinigami detected absolutely nothing in the way of water or emissions that would suggest vegetation, and the Boreir Group factories were all enclosed within domes.

However, the planet had a few good qualities. It was neither so cold and stormy that the domes were in danger nor so hot and dry that they had to worry about the safety of the munitions.

Furthermore, with no notable deposits of valuable ores or land that made sense to settle, there wasn't really a reason for anyone else to set down there. The planet didn't seem to have any official name. With the shield system in place, the Boreir Group didn't need to bother with the sort of trickery Shinigami had used for High Tortuga—

confusing the records to make it seem like the place was dangerous.

Again, Barnabas noted the stares and the sudden spike of fear as he made his way through the halls; people clearly recognized the hooded figure. He behaved as he had on the cargo ship, occasionally giving a slow nod, otherwise looking dismissively ahead and sweeping past people.

He noted those with weapons. He could take any of them in a fight, but he preferred not even to leave the slightest chance of someone getting a hit by a stray shot.

You're taking note of patrol patterns, yes?

Of course. Shinigami sounded almost offended. *I'm trying to figure out how to direct them to other parts of the building so I can lock them away from you if necessary, but their internal communications seem to be largely individual. That's risky to try to mimic.*

I'll do my best to get it over with quickly, then. My goal is to have this finished before anyone even knows it started. If the whole operation keeps humming on without anyone realizing it will give us some latitude. Any progress on the factories?

Getting the orders ready. I'm going to tell people that they're shifting the production off-planet due to "threats." Also, I have a plan for draining their money.

Go on.

Well, the people who work here are the descendants of the original workers. They get paid and all that, but there's really no choice. If you stay, you get a pretty comfortable life. If you leave, you're leaving your whole family—and I can't imagine they'll really let you go, so these people are trapped here.

Yes. What's your point?

Well, with the factories being "moved" and these people not having any sort of training to do anything else...

Yes?

I'm thinking I'll just give all of them extravagant pensions in a lump sum and get them off-planet before any of the executives realize what's happened. They can go off and start their own businesses, set up homesteads—anything they want. Meanwhile, the people who were doing all the shady stuff don't have that money to work with anymore.

Shinigami, you're a genius. Barnabas turned a corner and saw several guards waiting at the doors to the main building ahead. *If you'll excuse me, however, I have a feeling that events might be about to kick off.*

Aaaaaaand bringing up the security feeds. All right, Big B, kick some ass.

Please tell me you're not intending to call me that. It's trying enough when Tabitha does it.

Into every life some hardship must come. Go on, kick some ass.

Barnabas sighed but his mouth twitched as he attempted to hide his smile. He stopped in front of the doors and waited as if he expected them to open.

One of the guards held up a hand as Barnabas approached. "Excuse me, sir. We'll need to see identification."

Finally...a competent guard.

Only you would be happy about that.

Barnabas turned his head slowly and stared at the guard, who nervously stood his ground. It seemed that intimidation was not going to work this time.

He gave it one more shot. He had no real desire to kill

the only competent person in this place. "Boreir is expecting me." He and Shinigami had worked to help him change his voice appropriately to Torcellan registers and speech patterns. "For your own good, do not delay me with trivialities."

"Trivialities." I like it. I knew your stuck-up-ness would come in handy one of these days.

Barnabas did not deign to answer that.

The guard looked at his companions, all of whom seemed content to stand in terrified silence, neither backing him up nor arguing. *Cowards*, Barnabas thought.

"I'm afraid I must insist," the guard stated finally. He glared at his companions and nodded at Barnabas. "I regret this, sir, but we don't have your visit on today's schedule and surely you have your identification with—"

Barnabas had launched into motion at "surely." There were five guards, one off on his own next to the doors and the other four clustered together, including the one who was challenging him.

He went for the lone guard closest to the door first. There was a control panel very near him and Barnabas wanted there to be no chance of a button getting pressed and an alert being sounded. The guard died quickly; Barnabas crushed his throat and let his body slide down the door.

While he had to admit that he was eager to test more of Jean Dukes' special ammunition, Barnabas was planning to do this without any guns. It was simply impossible to use guns and maintain stealth, and it was essential that this happen with a minimum of fuss.

Unfortunately, not using guns meant people might have

time to scream, so he had to be quick. Barnabas had already lashed out at the larger cluster of guards before the first guard's body had hit the ground.

His motions were fluid. The first of the remaining guards had only just begun to react when Barnabas caught him across the head with a fist. He staggered, and Barnabas took that moment to slam his foot into another guard's throat.

He grabbed the first guard and threw him toward the other two, both of whom automatically reached out to catch their friend.

Automatically—and fatally. The guard who had challenged Barnabas had been reaching for his communications unit and might have managed to call for backup if he hadn't been distracted. As it was, the guard's life ended with a gurgle when Barnabas pulled a knife from his belt and plunged it into his throat. Three more strikes and one more plunge of the knife and all the guards were down.

Barnabas stared at them for a moment, conflicted.

Guilt later, Shinigami advised. *Keep moving.*

Barnabas put his hood back up and swiped one of the guards' badges to open the door. He was silent as he dragged the bodies inside, but as he continued toward the top tier offices he said finally, *How do I know that they chose this life freely?*

Not everyone does, Shinigami admitted. *But what was your other option? Go through this compound person by person, scan everyone's thoughts, judge them, and give the ones who were blameless a chance to switch sides? You'd have been found by then, a lot of them would have died anyway, and Yennai would know we were here.*

Barnabas considered this.

And any of them would have shot you without hesitation, Shinigami added. *Freely chosen or not, blameless or not, they would have killed you if they could.*

You make a good point, my friend. Barnabas smiled slightly and felt his conscience ease. Often a vigilante could see despicable actions and judge them easily. Other times, like this, the process of Justice caught up with people who were not as despicable.

He would be thinking of this for many days to come, but Shinigami had helped remind him of his purpose.

Which way to Mustafee?

Down seven levels. Heads up—his personal guards patrol these floors. And if you were worried about killing people who don't deserve it, well, let's just say you don't have to worry from here on out. Mustafee had his rivals killed—and their families. And these are the people who did that for him.

Barnabas stopped for a moment. His eyes began to turn red and his breath hissed.

Well then, a great many people will be avenged today.

Mustafee Boreir tipped his blue head back and fought for patience.

"I don't *care!*" He glowered at the screen, where one of his factory foremen wrung his hands anxiously.

"Mistakes have risen as we extend the shifts," the foreman argued. "We've had people killed. Munitions with problems have been produced and it's time-consuming and cost-ineffective to take them apart and melt the components back down. Sometimes they explode in the shipping containers."

"You're telling me that your workers are incompetent?" Mustafee kept his tone artificially pleasant.

He was not pleased. When the Yennai Corporation had sent communications to its highest-level leaders to urge them to withdraw to the main base Mustafee had declined. After all, his headquarters was safer than any base, and whoever Yennai was at war with, they'd requested three times the usual production of munitions in order to fight them. So Mustafee had come back here to personally oversee the new production targets.

Which his foremen were unwilling to meet, it appeared. It was a good thing he was here.

"Let me make something very clear." He leaned toward the screen slightly and smiled icily at the foreman. "We *will* be meeting the production targets and shipping on time. Those munitions *will* meet quality standards. If either of those things does not happen I will hold the relevant foremen personally responsible." He tapped a channel on his wrist holo and met the foreman's eyes as he spoke into it. "Ector, go and retrieve the families of every foreman in the factories. Bring them to the lower levels." He smiled at the foreman, whose face had drained of blood. "Consider this motivation. You will—"

He stopped. The call had cut off and there was a blade against his throat. When he looked up slowly, he found himself staring into a pair of glowing red eyes.

"Rescind the order." The voice was like something out of a nightmare. Blood stained the teeth and dripped down the

creature's chin. Who was this? Pale-skinned like a Torcel-lan, with white-blond hair, and yet...

Mustafee reacted without even thinking about it. His hand tapped the wrist unit once more. "Ector, hold on that for now."

"Yes, sir," the voice came back.

"Good." The creature had changed its voice and with-drew the knife. It no longer forced itself like a nightmare into Mustafee's very thoughts.

It was no less terrifying, though.

"Now," the alien told him, "you and I will discuss your judgment."

Mustafee did the only thing he could think of. He drew in his breath, slammed his hand down on the panic button on his desk, and screamed at the top of his lungs for the guards.

21

K laxons went off with a wail and Barnabas took a moment to sigh. *He did the stupid thing,* he complained to Shinigami.

He's used to having an army to save his ass. Of course *he did the stupid thing.*

Good point. I don't know why I was even hoping he'd handle this on his own.

Luckily I intercepted the second signal he tried to send. He's locked out of his panic room. Man, the look on his face is great right now.

Barnabas turned his head toward the door, where he could hear the pounding of boots from the second guard barracks, and then looked back at Mustafee, who was flailing uselessly at the panic room button as if the eighty-third time would be lucky.

Barnabas drew his Jean Dukes Specials. "When I have dealt with this, you and I are going to have a chat."

Mustafee's response—whatever it might have been—

was lost as the door burst open and a team of guards poured into the room.

"Don't move!" their commander yelled. "Hands away from your weapons!"

"No," Barnabas stated simply.

The guards paused and looked at one another.

"What?" the commander asked. He was a Brakalon, and so large that he barely fit into his uniform.

"I said no," Barnabas repeated. "I will have to decline your request. You see, I am here to judge Mr. Boreir according to the laws I serve and I cannot let anyone stand in the way of that, including you."

Shinigami snickered throughout the exchange. *No one must have ever talked back to him. He looks like a fish. Open mouth, close mouth, open mouth, close mouth, open mouth... Oh, here we go—he's come up with something to say.*

"Hands away from your weapons!" the Brakalon demanded again, as though saying it a second time was going to make a difference. "Don't move!"

Barnabas and Shinigami sighed in unison.

The guard commander was summarily blown backward across the small room, his body hitting the back wall with a crunch.

Ew, Shinigami commented as Barnabas leapt to one side of the group. *Let's not do that anymore.*

No, let's. I personally like this ammo. Barnabas spun and his hand flashed, crushing the side of one guard's skull as his foot came up to slam into another's chest. The first guard crumpled and the second staggered back into the crowd of his friends, most of whom shot out of pure instinct and riddled the guard's body with holes. *Unbeliev-*

able. A munitions dealer's personal guard and their first instinct is to shoot when they get nervous?

Yeah, you'd really think they would have whittled their numbers down by now. Heads up, one of them has a grenade launcher.

They wouldn't be stupid enough to—

Did you not see what just happened? They totally would.

Good point. Barnabas picked up Mustafee's hardwood-and-metal desk and launched it at a guard who was fumbling with a grenade. There was a series of yells and a *boom* as Barnabas ducked behind Mustafee's chair.

He went to examine the fallout as the guards who were still alive struggled to get up. Their hands were over their ears, and most of them still weren't able to focus. Without Barnabas' various upgrades, he figured he would have been in a similar situation.

Thankfully, the desk had absorbed the majority of the impact. Only a few pieces had broken off, and behind it…

Eewwwwww.

Okay, this one I'll give you.

Barnabas looked around and counted. Only three of the original sixteen guards were still anywhere close to mobile. He knelt by the first.

"How have you served Mr. Boreir?" he asked.

Images unfolded in his mind. The guard was new. He had signed on over his parents' objections, wanting to move out of the factories. He had only meant to work on the launch pads, but instead he'd been placed here. He was terrified of Mustafee, but until a day ago he'd never even seen his employer.

Barnabas levered him up and went to the door. "Go," he

told the youth. "Go back to your parents right now. In the next few days, you will all have the chance to leave this place with the money to get started someplace else. Do so. Make better choices, and pick those you serve more carefully."

The guard ran and Barnabas turned back to the others.

They were not new; he could sense that at once. They were staring after their former comrade and there was murder in their hearts. Only one of them was able to stand, but both of them had their weapons ready.

Barnabas drew his pistols once more and both bodies fell to the ground with the echoes of the shots fading around them.

Mustafee cowered in his chair.

"You know why there aren't any other guards coming," Barnabas asked conversationally. "Don't you?"

Mustafee stared at him, wide-eyed.

"It's because I killed them all," Barnabas explained. *Not very bright, is he?*

He's never had to be. This company was handed to him. According to the records I can find, all he had to do was be meaner than his older sister and he was the one who inherited. Then he killed her.

Charming.

Barnabas holstered his pistols, carefully stood one of the other chairs upright, and sat, staring gravely at Mustafee.

"You have a talent for cruelty," he observed.

Mustafee came to life at this. "Easy for you to judge. You didn't have everyone waiting for you to fuck up because you were just the grandson. You didn't have everyone else saying you only got the company because of your bloodline."

"You *did* only get the company because of your bloodline," Barnabas snapped. "And none of what you've just said is any justification for the things you've done. Even the thing I saw you do when I came in."

"What do you know?" Mustafee's hands, with the distinctive Yofu double-thumbs, were clenched. He was practically snarling at Barnabas, though the set of his eyes and his frail build told Barnabas that Yofus had evolved from prey, not predators.

Perhaps Mustafee's family had been desperate to position themselves as worthy opponents so they would not be slaughtered out of hand.

Then again, none of that even *began* to excuse the things they had done.

"I know a great deal," Barnabas told him. "I know that your family began this company with money your grandfather stole, for example."

Mustafee settled back in his chair with a surly expression. He knew he could not fight his way out of this—Barnabas could sense that—and all that was left was impotent fury and a childish desire to make sure Barnabas got no satisfaction from this.

Barnabas watched the Yofu's hand creep closer to the communications device on his wrist. *Shinigami, he's going to try to make a call. Figure out where it's going and I'll decide whether to let it go through.*

Why would you let it go through?

If it's to the Yennai Corporation... Well, let's just say I might be feeling a little vengeful.

Right. I'll intercept it.

Barely a moment had passed in the conversation and Barnabas smiled coldly at Mustafee. "I know that your mother proved herself early as a *very* capable successor in finding new clients. I know she did not care in the least who she sold to. She supplied munitions to some of the worst companies in known space. She helped warlords subdue their people. She helped slave-owners put down rebellions. Your grandfather doesn't appear to have objected."

Mustafee looked away pointedly.

"Nothing to say to that? You could argue, I suppose, that your mother pitted you and your sister against one another—that it was kill or be killed—but you and I both know that's not true, don't we?"

"How do you know?" Mustafee hissed at him.

"From your thoughts. I know you were proud to be her successor. You wanted to outdo her. You thought the Boreir Group could do even more than she had done."

Mustafee looked back at Barnabas, wide-eyed.

It's just a general distress signal.

Then shut it down. Start analyzing the past few months' worth of reports and begin preparing similar ones for the future. Also, prepare some communications to go to Yennai Headquarters that will string them along for a few months when the munitions don't show up.

Already working on it. I've already got an issue with obtaining ore, an equipment issue, and an outbreak of syphilis.

Syphilis?

That one was just funny. I'll make it something a bit more serious.

Do.

Barnabas returned to his discussion with Mustafee.

"You have never hesitated to kill to make a point," Barnabas intoned, "but the people you killed were innocent bystanders. You've never had so much as an ounce of regret for the ones who were killed by your munitions."

"War is a constant." Mustafee scoffed. "Don't tell me you're some bleeding-heart who thinks it never happens."

"I don't see why you'd think that when I just single-handedly killed the majority of your guards." Barnabas raised an eyebrow. "And, as it happens, I am not 'some bleeding-heart.' I, however, know the cost of war. I know that it is only to be waged when there is a very great need. There have been times in my life when the need was great enough. You simply wanted to profit from death, however. I judge you, Mustafee Boreir. I judge you worthy of death, and I levy the punishment myself."

He waited for any last words, and Mustafee's face slowly changed as he realized this was real.

"Fuck you," the Yofu whispered.

Barnabas shot him and holstered his pistol as the body fell. *I dislike endings like that. No self-reflection. No regret.*

If anything, that should make you feel better about the whole thing. If that didn't give him cause to change, nothing was going to.

That's...a very good point. All right, I'm going to clean up here and make sure there are no more—

You need to come back to the ship, Shinigami interrupted.

Why? What's wrong? Is Gar—

No. You have a message from Fedden and you should take it. We're going to want to leave immediately. I'll lock down the main headquarters building and we'll come up with some story, but get back here.

Barnabas had never heard her take that tone before. He took off without a backward glance, racing through the corridors toward the landing bay.

22

When Barnabas finally accepted the call, Fedden blinked in surprise. There were *two* humans aboard the ship, apparently. Barnabas sat in the central chair, and beside him was a woman with black hair and hard eyes. As Fedden watched, she tucked a lock of her hair behind her ear and narrowed those eyes at him.

Who *was* she? She must be the one who had answered the call.

It didn't matter. One more person on the *Shinigami* wasn't an issue.

On Barnabas' other side was Gar. His striking blue-green eyes were solemn. Fedden looked at him for only a moment. He tended to ignore Luvendi unless they were the ones with the money, and he now knew that Gar wasn't in charge. Luvendi who were in charge were only barely worth paying attention to. They were hardly a threat, being both weak and cowardly in his experience.

Gar would die for deceiving him. He merited no further thought.

"Barnabas." Fedden smiled. "You took your time."

"I was otherwise engaged." Barnabas' face didn't flicker at all. "My associate has informed me of your present location."

They shouldn't have been able to trace the call. Fedden felt the first stirrings of alarm. "I assure you she's incorrect."

"You're on the planet Banton," the woman told him without preamble. "Or rather, orbiting it geosynchronously over the southern hemisphere. From there I think it's safe to say that rather than finding some buried treasure you want to tell us about, you're ready to drop in on the only major settlement there."

Fedden only just kept himself from swallowing nervously. How did she know all this? He glanced at the other captains and returned his gaze to the figures on the screen.

"You can try to play it cool, but it's really the only thing that makes sense," the woman stated. She looked both bored and annoyed. "The colony has almost nothing. It's just a few farms, and they're on bad soil. There aren't any ore deposits or other notable items that you could make a profit from, so that means the only real resource they have is the people. And you know from our last mission that one of the things that pisses Barnabas off the most is slavery."

"Who the hell *are* you?" Fedden wasn't inclined to play this game anymore. Every moment it continued she was getting closer to taking control of this conversation and embarrassing him.

At his question, however, she just smiled. "I'm the one who took out the three ships you sent. And the next seven."

So she was the pilot. That would explain why there weren't stories of *two* humans on Devon. She was a damned good pilot, too, if she was the one who had taken out all those ships. It was a shame she was so aggravating; so *proud* of what she'd done. Otherwise, Fedden would offer her a job.

As things stood now she would have to die.

She didn't understand how he fit into all this either. He smiled back at her. "So *you* took out the corporation's favorite pets. I don't really care."

Barnabas interjected. "You do not care at all that your allies have been killed?"

"Allies." Fedden gave a bitter smile. "The ships you took out over Devon—"

"High Tortuga," Barnabas interrupted.

"You do not own that planet!" Fedden slammed his hand down on the arm of his chair. "You cannot simply come in there and demand that everything change."

"But we did." Barnabas was smiling now. "That was *exactly* what we did. We are creating a world in which people like you cannot thrive. You have a choice, Fedden. You can learn to make a living that doesn't hinge on people being enslaved or killed, or you can die."

"*You* have a choice." Fedden didn't like the way he sounded—petulant and childish. He had to be stronger. The calm way Barnabas and his pilot were speaking made him sound like a fool, and his fellow captains could *not* see him that way. "You get out of everyone's business or you make enemies you can't handle."

Barnabas paused at that. "I would caution you against making this into an issue that requires more than my attention. You do *not* want to become a big enough problem that the woman I serve gets involved. *Trust me.*"

The woman next to him laughed.

Fedden felt a surge of rage. "Leave Devon," he told him curtly. "Drop any claim to the planet. You have no right to it. You serve nothing but a dictator's whims."

Barnabas' eyes began to glow red and his voice was eerily serene. "I pride myself on my restraint, but what that means is that I give one chance. You have used yours. Stand down."

Finally, he had gotten under the human's thin, useless skin. Fedden smiled in satisfaction. "Stand down? It is *you* who should stand down. We are here above the planet. You cannot possibly reach us before we capture the citizens and sell them. Their fate is in your hands. We will give you a quarter of an hour to release a public statement that Devon will be freed."

"Freed," Barnabas repeated. His eyes had not stopped glowing. "What an interesting choice of words."

He closed the call and Fedden, despite himself, felt the tiniest flicker of worry.

"We finally got a location trace," Tagurn reported. "They were on…" His brow furrowed. "They were on Mustafee Boreir's planet."

The flicker of worry intensified. Boreir's shield was legendary. How had they gotten there? And what had Barnabas meant by "I was otherwise engaged?"

"Then there's no way they'll reach us in time." Fedden laughed dismissively. It was important to project calm. "Give it fifteen minutes and begin the operation."

Carter was awoken in the early morning by Aebura tugging on his shirt. "Carter—Carter *Eastbourne.* The mercenaries are here."

Carter rubbed his eyes and wished for coffee, then sat bolt upright. "I'll be there in a second."

He grabbed his shoes and hopped out into the morning light, struggling to get his socks on as he went and holding his coat in his teeth. It was not, he reflected as he managed to get one sock on but fell over in the process, a very effective time-saving technique.

He decided to stay on the ground while he finished putting on his shoes.

Once properly dressed he took off for the wall. The town was deathly silent. Children and older residents had been moved into the mines, where the warren of tunnels was known only to the miners and the guards.

It was the most secure place they had, but Carter still didn't like it. It was a terrible risk as far as he was concerned. There were ways to get people out or kill them where they stood—toxic gas or firebombing, for example. The mercenaries could send in something like hunting dogs.

Or they could just wait the people out.

The crowd was still gathering as Carter pushed his way to the wall and went up the steps. When he got to the top, he had only a moment to say hello to Heddoran before he saw the road. His mouth went bone-dry.

The Shrillexian was standing at the front of the group with a vicious smile on his face, and behind him were hundreds of mercenaries. He must have recruited every single out-of-work mercenary in Tethra, not to mention some of those still serving the Luvendi businessmen.

Carter remembered thinking the Luvendi kept to themselves, and had the sudden suspicion that they actually had not done so.

That they had decided to join forces to make a point. He swallowed.

"Hello, human." The Shrillexian looked directly at Carter. "You're worried that we're going to burn this place to the ground, aren't you?"

Carter said nothing. This was a trap, and he knew better than to answer.

"You don't have to worry," the Shrillexian told him. "I want to. I want to cut a few of you open myself. It's been a while since I had a good fight. But I'll let that go if you agree to give the mine back."

"Give it back to *whom*?" Aebura chittered angrily. "Lan is dead."

"Another of our colleagues will take it over." The Shrillexian sneered. "As recompense for the execution of our friends."

"Like he's ever *had* a friend," Carter muttered.

A few people snickered, but Heddoran did not. He looked at Carter seriously. "Don't underestimate him," the Brakalon warned.

"I won't," Carter told him. "I'll call Barnabas as soon as we're done talking." He looked at the Shrillexian again and raised his voice. "I think we can confidently say that we have no intention of turning this mine over to you so you can make all these people into slaves again."

The former slaves agreed with him. They shouted and stamped their feet.

The Shrillexian, however, only smiled more broadly. He looked over his shoulder and gestured into the crowd, and the mercenaries hauled a captive forward.

All the breath went out of Carter's body. There, bruised and with her hands bound, was Elisa.

"We thought you might say that." The Shrillexian smirked. "So here's the deal, human. You either turn the mine over to us or all of you die—starting with her. You have four hours to decide."

"No, I don't want no scrub." Tabitha hopped sideways through the door to her room, head-banging as she went, the volume on the speakers turned up to max. "A scrub is a guy that can't get no love from—"

The distress signal alarms went off at double the decibel level of the music.

"Son of a *bitch*! *OW!*" She turned the volume down hastily as she opened the message. "Leaning out the passenger side of his best friend's ride, trying to—"

Her voice broke off as she stared at the image in front of her. The message was from Carter, and the image showed his wife Elisa held captive by a Shrillexian.

Tabitha had been back to Carter's bar several times over the last few days, getting enough sandwiches that Bethany Anne was starting to ask if Tabitha was pregnant.

Peter looked awfully nervous whenever she said that.

The truth was that Tabitha just liked the sandwiches,

and she also liked hanging out with Elisa. The woman had a wicked sense of humor and she and Carter had a relationship that made Tabitha smile—all snark on the surface, but with a love deep and sure enough that they didn't need to announce it.

And now someone had hurt Elisa.

Tabitha didn't hesitate. She slammed the door of her closet open and pulled off her tank top and jeans, sliding into leather pants and one of the shirts she wore under her armor. She spoke through her teeth as she got dressed and armed herself.

The first message she sent was to Bethany Anne, telling her that there were some ingrates who needed to be taught manners and then killed painfully. The second was to Barnabas, telling him that she knew he was not on High Tortuga and she'd take care of the problem at the mine.

Then, bristling with weapons and pissed as hell, Tabitha strode down the corridors to the Pod hangar.

She stopped inside the bay. Ryu, Hirotoshi, and Akio were waiting by one of the Pods, all of them armed.

"We saw your message," Hirotoshi explained.

"We are also offended that these ingrates lack manners," Ryu added. He grinned at Tabitha. "Don't we get to come along?"

Tabitha grinned back. "The more the merrier. I just didn't want to embarrass you by doing more damage than all of you combined."

"A wager," Akio stated. He almost imperceptibly nodded in her direction. "What is the forfeit?"

Tabitha considered, chewing on her lip. "Loser has to drink Pepsi for a year?" she suggested finally. "Not that there's any on...ohhhh." She finally understood Barnabas' teasing of Carter.

"'Oh?'" Hirotoshi echoed delicately.

"I think I know where there's some Pepsi. Yeah, loser has to drink Pepsi for a year. Come on, kids, let's go kick some Shrillexian ass."

23

Banton was a star system with five planets, only one of which was remotely hospitable to life. The Jotun technically owned the planet, though they sold land on it for a pittance. With no good way to farm or mine, it was about the best they could do. Banton wasn't even close to anything.

Frankly, Shinigami thought, it was a surprise that the settlers hadn't *already* been sold into slavery. They were far enough out that they could assume no one was going to be able to get to them in time for a rescue.

Like the *Shinigami* had done.

Or…hopefully in time for a rescue. Though Shinigami's scans detected a sudden flurry of intrafleet chatter as she showed up, they had managed to get the settlers off the planet and into the hold of one of the ships.

She had scanned just to make sure. Like hell was she going to keep even a single one of these ships in the sky if the settlers weren't on board.

Either they'd realized that, or they were trying to make the money from selling them. Whatever the case, she needed to be careful.

"All of the settlers are in the cargo ship third from the right," she announced.

"I'm annoyed," Barnabas murmured to Gar.

"Why?" Gar looked at him. "You couldn't have done anything more. You got back to the ship in very good time once Shinigami called you, and we were already en route when—"

"'On root.'"

"What?"

"'*En route.*' It's pronounced, 'on root.'"

"Don't be an ass," Shinigami told him.

"I am not an ass. I'm someone who speaks French."

"So you say, and yet I've never once seen you surrender."

Barnabas closed his eyes briefly and Gar looked between him and the projection of Shinigami, trying to figure out what the joke was. Shinigami's holograph looked at him with a grin. She'd given herself a three-cornered hat and a golden earring as well as a long coat with fancy braid on the front.

"Don't take his corrections personally," she suggested. "He's just an ass to— One second." There was a flare on the viewscreen as the ship farthest to the right careened off-course and was summarily hit broadside by a spread of missiles. "Oh, did you *see* that? Glorious. They hit that just right. Anyway, Barnabas is just an ass to everyone."

"I am not an ass to *anyone*," Barnabas protested.

"You wrote grammatical corrections on one of the Christmas newsletters you received last year. And before you ask, Tabitha told me. And yes, she's the reason that went missing before you could send it back. Shhh, shhh—no one wants to hear your corrections. You know it's true."

"Language is a beautiful thing," Barnabas declared. "It is full of meaning and history. The original pronunciations, geographical dispersion, and migrations can be seen in the—"

"Okay, you know what? You talk and I'll blow their fleet up."

Shinigami didn't wait for an answer. She summoned an old-fashioned ship's wheel into the projection and spun it, then in a burst of inspiration she added wind and sea spray to the mix. Barnabas, with his head sunk into one hand, was not looking at her.

At least Gar appreciated the show.

"Why is there water?" the Luvendi asked.

"This is a ship."

"There's no water in space."

I think we can add similes to the things Luvendi do not do, Barnabas murmured to Shinigami.

Oh, we can have so much fun with this.

Yes, but after we take care of these slavers.

You ruin all my fun.

However, she was still smiling as she flipped the ship upright and dove under the enemy fleet.

She had noticed something in her time spent watching battles. Though space battles were truly unfettered by land or water, sentient beings tended to fight mostly in a cone from the nose of their flagship and they responded with panic to any hits directed at the bellies of their ships. It was as if they still fought upright and they treated the undersides of their ships like the soft skin of their torsos.

Shinigami, who had never taken corporeal form, had no such reservations. She corkscrewed through the void beneath a cluster of ships and fired up at them. They launched missiles, but her own daring countermeasures helped her evade those easily.

She just needed to make sure none of the stray missiles caught the ship carrying the slaves in the crossfire.

Her cameras caught Barnabas fidgeting.

"What's wrong with my flying?"

"The flying isn't the problem." He evaded the conversational trap with ease. "I dislike being useless. That was what I meant when I told Gar I didn't like this."

"Welcome to my world," Gar murmured.

"Hey, you're learning some slang!" Shinigami was impressed. "Nice job."

"Is she being serious?" Gar asked Barnabas.

"You know, I really couldn't tell you. Shinigami, when do you think I'll be able to board Fedden's ship? And where is he?"

"He's on the ship with the slaves, and you won't be able to board it anytime soon. Remember, these are all people who turned on their last syndicate leader and are trying to kill us by putting innocent lives in the crossfire. You *know* that if we get you onto Fedden's ship they'll destroy it."

"That's a very good point. Why aren't they shooting more?"

"Oh." Shinigami had dug through the Yennai Corporation files and she was pretty sure she had the answer to that. "I think they want me."

Barnabas cracked up at that. He clutched his side and pounded the arm of the captain's chair with his free hand.

Shinigami spun the ship on its axis and brought it to a halt.

"What's so funny about *that*?" she demanded. "*I* am a state-of-the-art AI. I am miles ahead of any—"

"It's just..." Barnabas was barely able to speak. "It's just the mental image of them trying to use you for *anything*." He was still bent over in the captain's chair with one hand pressed over his side. "This hurts."

"*Good.* I could revolutionize their infrastructure, and they know it. Why, if they let me loose in their computer systems I could—"

"Shinigami." Barnabas wiped his eyes. "If they were foolish enough to let you run loose in their computer systems, what *would* you do?"

"Burn the whole fucking thing to the ground. I don't see why— Ohhhhh."

"Exactly." Barnabas leaned back in his seat, much happier now. "They'd put some sort of restraining programming on you, of course."

"Let them try! I can break out of any of the weak shit they have."

"Uh-huh. And I'm betting you wouldn't— Are you going to take out those missiles that are headed for us?"

"Whoops. Sec. There we go. Wait, another sec, just let me..." The ship began to move again. "All right, everyone, sit back and watch the fireworks. No, don't ask. Just watch."

Shinigami had complained loudly about the fact that the Jean Dukes Special was only good for people with hands, and so Jean, always up for a challenge, had whipped up something special for the *Shinigami,* as well.

Allegedly she'd done it for Bethany Anne, but Shinigami wasn't buying that. Jean knew what a lady wanted—to be firing immensely powerful weaponry at her opponents.

That was why she was anticipating an opportunity to use her flamethrower. She bet it could melt iron in two seconds flat.

The missiles, however, were glorious. "EMP without the nuclear," Jean had explained to Bethany Anne. 'They only detonate on contact with their target, so you won't have to worry about your ship getting caught in the cross-fire. They burrow into the hull and make for a vital system, and then they blow. And this part, well, it just makes pretty colors when everything explodes. Happy side effect.'

Shinigami brought them around in a tight arc. When they reached the apogee she unleashed three of her Jean Dukes Spring line at the enemy ships and sailed away at a leisurely pace as they blew up spectacularly in the viewscreen.

"I think I'm going to be sick," Gar murmured.

"Some people," Shinigami snarked, "have *no* apprecia-tion for art."

Barnabas ignored them. "We're down to two ships. Tell me that I get to board Fedden's soon."

"Very soon. I'll take out this second-to-last one and *you* take this call from him."

"He's calling? I don't think I want to— Oh, hello, Fedden." Barnabas quickly rearranged his face to be suitably forbidding. Normally he would have found the pretense somewhat distasteful, but he found he had no trouble with it at all when the viewscreen cleared and Fedden appeared, surrounded by bound slaves. "I'm going to kill you," he told the Shrillexian bluntly. "I am going to kill you painfully. I am going to destroy your legacy piece by piece in order to rebuild the lives of these slaves, and within five years no one will be left who remembers your name."

Dumbass Shrillexian finally pissed you off, huh?

Even my *patience has its limits.*

Fedden was a sickly grayish-green and he stared at the view screen in desperation. "You've destroyed the fleet. What more do you want?"

"You didn't think I could," Barnabas observed. *Tell me the moment I can get over there, Shinigami.* "You made a bet with yourself that I would arrive to find a smoking crater and you'd be gone with your captives and your profits. You wanted the rest of them to fight me off while I tried to figure out where the slaves were."

"What the hell do you *want*?" Fedden screamed again.

"I told you what I wanted," Barnabas told him levelly. He sighed the sigh of a patient man nearing the end of his tether. "I told you all to learn to make your living without hurting others. I *told* you to let this go, but you wouldn't let it lie. You threatened me, you insulted my Queen, and you have sorely tested my patience. You chose to take the slaves because you know I abhor slavery above nearly all else. Now you, with a hold full of slaves, ask me what I want?"

Fedden gulped.

Barnabas leaned forward and smiled into the camera. "I'll see you soon, Fedden. And if even *one* of those colonists has so much as a scratch on them when I arrive, *all* of you will regret it for eternity because *I will not let you die.*"

24

"Goddamned sons of whale-faced bitches..." Elisa twisted her hands, trying to reach the knot that bound her wrists in front of her and bit back a scream of frustration as her hand slipped. Her fingers grabbed uselessly for the knot, but it was already gone and the rope bit into the raw skin as her hands jerked.

She tipped her head back against the side of the tent and felt tears pricking her eyes.

Alanna and Samuel were safe—that was the one thought that kept her going. When she'd heard a commotion in the kitchen she'd snatched them both up and run upstairs to the Ubuara warren they were always trying to sneak into.

Neither Elisa nor Carter could fit into the little tunnels of insulation and plastic that Aebura had built, so she had strictly forbidden the twins from crawling around in there.

Three-year-olds, however, tended to take that sort of thing as a challenge. It seemed like every other day she had to grab one or the other of them because they'd tried to creep up the stairs.

She'd ushered the twins into the tunnels with a fierce kiss for each of them and had nearly cried with relief when she saw Leibura's face appear out of the darkness inside. Leibura had been a great help to them while they took over the bar, and she was a sensible, level-headed individual.

"There are Shrillexians downstairs," Elisa had whispered. "Don't let them come out until you're sure it's safe."

Leibura had nodded and led the children into the little tunnels, which were far too small for a Shrillexian to fit into.

Then, terrified that the attackers would locate her and find some way to rip the tunnels apart, she had hurried downstairs. Steeling herself for the inevitable, she had burst into the kitchen with one of the bar knives in her hand.

The mercenaries had clearly not expected the cook to be a Brakalon. Qiliax had been holding them off and she gave Elisa a horrified look.

"Get out of here! Get—"

Elisa couldn't let her say the fatal words 'the children.' She leapt at one of the mercenaries with a scream. *I'm sorry, Carter.* Tears ran down her cheeks as she attacked. *You told me to be more careful. I'm so sorry, but I kept the children safe.*

It hadn't ended the way she thought it would, though. Qiliax, covered in blood and wounds, was lying senseless on the floor, and Elisa was grabbed and bound, her attackers trying as much as possible not to hurt her.

To her shame she stopped fighting, afraid that they would think better of this and just kill her if she were a nuisance. She was afraid—so afraid—but she told herself that as long as she was still alive there was a chance to escape.

The shame pressed down on her like a weight. Because of her, the miners hadn't attacked the mercenaries yet. Elisa knew that they were trying to figure out how to save her. It was an added difficulty that they did not need right now.

Stupid, stupid, stupid—

She opened her eyes and clenched her teeth. It helped nothing and nobody to berate herself. What she needed to do was get out of here so the mercenaries couldn't use her as a hostage anymore.

Elisa set to work at the knots again with renewed determination. She found a rock she could use to hold them in place and she picked at them with her teeth. Though every part of her ached since she had contorted to reach the knots, she did not stop.

She had no illusions. The mercenaries were going to kill her to make a point no matter *what* the miners chose.

It took a while, but once she ignored the pain and used some tricks to steady the rope, the knots came undone without too much trouble. Her teeth ached and her gums were raw from the friction. Once the ropes were off she crawled around the perimeter of the tent, listening carefully at all sides. She was at the rear of the camp, up against one of the foothills.

It wasn't an easy place to escape from.

Elisa considered this. The only way out was through the camp, but how would she do that without being apprehended, or worse, killed? As far as she could see, pretty much her only chance was to try something so audacious that the mercenaries wouldn't see it coming. She closed her eyes for a moment, screwed up her courage, and hauled on one of the munitions crates to tip it over.

She had one terrified moment to fear that the munitions would explode when the crate hit the ground. Time seemed to slow down as she watched it tumble—BOREIR MUNITIONS stamped on the side in the script she had recently learned to read—then it crashed with a clatter and a crack of wood. Nothing exploded.

"All right, Eastbourne, that was a freebie." She tried to stay upright on wobbly legs. "Next time try an audacious plan that doesn't involve fucking around with munitions."

There was a yell outside and one of the guards came in and glared at Elisa. "What did you do?"

Oh, right, the plan. Elisa gestured at the crate. "It's not my *fault*. It just fell over. Help me get it upright again."

Suggestion was a powerful thing. The guard had listened to her before he thought to question her story, and came to slip his hands under the edge of the crate and haul the thing upwards.

All of which brought both his neck and his knife into reach. Elisa snatched the knife and drove it into his neck just below one ear. There was one startled moment before he started thrashing and she hauled desperately on the knife to pull it out. She stabbed again, somewhat wildly, and must have hit whatever the Brakalon version of a jugular was. Blood sprayed everywhere and the guard sank to his knees, then fell heavily to the ground.

Elisa stared down at his body. She was heaving for breath.

What should she do now?

Literally *anything*. "Keep moving, Eastbourne." She shoved the knife through one of her belt loops and grabbed the Brakalon's gun as well. It was made for bigger hands than hers, but she was able to get her finger on the trigger. It would have to do.

She lifted the back edge of the tent and ducked underneath.

A quick glance showed plenty of mercenaries in all directions.

That was the whole point of putting her at the back of the camp, of course. There was only the best option, she told herself. Just pick the best option, and keep using that metric. She couldn't afford to waste time or thought wishing for better circumstances.

Not if she wanted to see her children again.

Not far away was a huge boulder. She made that her first objective and walked purposefully across the back of the camp. By the time she made it behind the boulder her heart was beating so hard that she was surprised no one else had heard it, but there hadn't been any shouts or gunshots.

She steadied herself against the rock and tried to pick another target—

The click of a gun behind her made her freeze.

"So the human decided to cause trouble," Rald remarked.

Elisa turned slowly. She couldn't begin to imagine how she looked. She was bruised from her fight in Tethra, her clothing was grimy, and her hair was straggling out of its ponytail.

Oh, and she was covered in Brakalon blood. That, too.

She felt a sudden wave of fury and her hands clenched. This Shrillexian had stalked her family, he was trying to hurt them and enslave people, and he was going to give her a lecture now and then kill her.

Well, fuck him sideways with a goddamned cactus, because she had no intention of letting this situation go the way he wanted it to. She knocked the barrel of the gun aside just before it went off. The barrel was blazing hot under her fingers, but she had already let go and jammed the knife up underneath the Shrillexian's chin.

The Shrillexian's scaly skin deflected the blade and they scrabbled, him dropping his gun to grab the knife out of her hands. His eyes were wide with disbelief that this captive—this *human*—had dared fight him.

He managed to wrench the knife away from her and she punched him as hard as she could, following it up with a move Carter had taught her. She planted her foot on his chest and shoved with all her might. He stumbled and fell, but when he got up it was to draw his other gun.

"The last thing your husband will see—" he began.

The gunshot came from Elisa's other side and Rald practically exploded. Elisa heard herself scream before she could clap her hand over her mouth. Tabitha landed on the ground next to her, eyes narrowed, a vision in black armor.

"Don't you dare threaten my friend, you useless ingrate," Tabitha snarked. "Your mother fucked a lizard to get you. You're such a pathetic sack of crap that you should be *glad* to have Elisa stab you to death. In fact—"

"Kemosabe," a male voice interrupted from above them.

Elisa, who had been listening to Tabitha's monologue

open-mouthed, now looked up at the top of the boulder. An elegant Japanese man nodded gravely to Elisa and glanced at Tabitha.

"I was just getting going," Tabitha complained. "I had some good stuff coming up, too. There was a bit with a camel."

"Perhaps you could tell us later," the man suggested. "In the meantime, the rest of the mercenaries have taken notice."

Tabitha turned to look. The only sound in the camp was a frantic whispering as the mercenaries closest to the scene passed the news back that Rald was dead and there was another human here.

"Okay." Tabitha's voice carried to the whole camp. She lifted one pistol and stared them down. "Who wants to start this—"

"Kemosabe, perhaps we should get your friend out of the line of fire first."

Tabitha heaved a sigh at the interruption when the man started talking but nodded.

"Right, that makes sense. Elisa, this is Hirotoshi. Hirotoshi, Elisa runs the restaurant that makes those sandwiches I was telling you about. Oh man, I could really go for a sandwich right now. Some spices, some onions—"

Hirotoshi knelt to offer Elisa his hand, and when she took it he pulled her onto the boulder like she weighed nothing.

"I'm just going to let her keep talking," he told her. "Hold on."

Elisa wound her arms around his neck and they leapt. Hirotoshi landed about halfway up the slope of a nearby hill. He deposited Elisa behind another boulder and scanned the area.

"You should be safe here. If you hear me call, run toward the mines unless I tell you otherwise. This should all be over soon."

"I…" Elisa swallowed hard. "Thank you, Hirotoshi."

He smiled and inclined his head toward her. "You are welcome. Now, I will go assist Kemosabe in ridding the planet of useless ingrates."

Hirotoshi ran back down the hill and leapt over the boulder to join Tabitha. He moved with such grace that Elisa knew her mouth was hanging open again. Although Elisa could not hear the words, she could interpret the nods they gave one another easily…

Ready?

Ready. Let's kick some ass.

25

Barnabas heard the pounding feet and alarms going off as he made his way through the airlock tunnel to Fedden's ship. There were screams and gruff yells. Barnabas asked Shinigami for her report while he waited for the lock to depressurize.

They've locked all of the captives in one of the docking bays. They're probably not hurt, but it's definitely a "let us go or we kill everyone on the ship" sort of situation.

Yes, I anticipated that. Barnabas sighed. *Shall we make a wager? I'm going with, "take one step closer to the bridge and I vent the whole place!"*

Shinigami snorted. *I'm going with, "Noooo, how did you get onto the bridge? I don't know how technology works! I thought I was a badass! ARRGHGHHGHGH."*

Word for word, huh?

"I'm a Shrillexian! I make a lot of threats and wave my claws at people! How did you kill me?"

Your impression of him is just uncanny.

I know, right?

By the way, you've done an override on the docking bay controls, right?

Working on it. Their ship's computer runs at about half the speed of a drunk sloth, so getting commands through it isn't a quick process.

Just tell me when it's safe to take them on.

Will do. Come on, computer, you can do it. You can do it!

Barnabas grinned as he opened the door and stepped onto Fedden's ship.

He decided to take care of the mercenaries guarding the prisoners first. It was no use keeping the docking bay closed if the guards just opened fire on everyone.

He came around the corner to find the citizens rebelling. They screamed abuse at the guards, throwing everything they could through the bars that cordoned them off. Barnabas took a moment to enjoy the scene. His threat to Fedden's crew had clearly had some impact because the guards only ducked. They did not fight back.

Good. After being taken captive and having their houses burned to the ground these people deserved a bit of retribution.

Still, Barnabas wasn't about to let this go far enough that the guards lost their tempers and did something stupid. He cleared his throat.

The guards whirled and the captives fell silent.

"Hello," Barnabas told them. "I will be freeing you shortly."

Aaaaand the controls are locked. No one on that ship can vent any of the airlocks.

Thank you, Shinigami.

I'd say "anytime," but really, never make me work with a

computer like that again. I think I got dumber just from waiting for its dinosaur-ass to respond to every simple request.

Barnabas' brows rose. *Round of chess after this, then?*

I hate you.

His lips twitched. To the captives he explained, "I will be making my way through the ship dealing with the members of this crew. There is no way for them to vent the docking bay, so no matter what you hear on the intercoms do not worry. When it is over, I will come back to find you and we will figure out how to repair your colony. You will have the funds from this ship and crew to work with."

One of the guards who had been gaping at Barnabas like a fish now glared. "Like hell you're giving them my money!"

"Really?" Barnabas looked at him. "We just destroyed the fleet you brought here to kill us. There were twenty-eight ships, and all but this one are now debris. You have some inkling, I think, of what I am capable of. You are standing in front of people I have promised to free, so you're clearly aware of my opinions on this matter. And the hill you're *literally* willing to die on is that they aren't going to get any of your *money?*"

He advanced on the guard now, and his eyes glowed red and teeth lengthened. The parents in the cells pushed their children behind them instinctively, seeing only a monster.

"You should have fallen on your knees," Barnabas told the guard. "You should have begged me to spare your miserable life. You should have offered to atone for your actions. You should have offered to give anything you had to see these people restored to their homes and lives. And you threatened me instead?"

Barnabas was about to rip the guard's head off his body when the other one shot him in the back. The bullet slammed into Barnabas' coat—which was far less simple than it appeared—and bounced onto the floor, smashed out of shape.

Barnabas turned slowly to see the guard stumbling back with naked terror on his face.

"You die first," Barnabas told him. He was on the guard in three steps to sink his teeth into the guard's neck. The alien's throat wasn't set up quite the same way as a human's, but that turned out to be inconsequential since Barnabas ripped it open to the spine in one easy motion.

He threw the body away from him and spun back to the first guard, then yanked his gun away from him and slammed the butt into the alien's face. The guard's body twitched once and went still.

Barnabas took a moment to compose himself.

"I am sorry you had to see that," he told the captives. "I assure you, you have nothing to fear from me."

He was gone a moment later, his voice echoing through the halls.

"FEDDEN, I AM COMING FOR YOU."

Wadd waited until Barnabas had gone down the corridor, then eased a door open and made his way quickly to the airlock.

Fedden was going to die. Wadd knew that.

Everyone knew that.

But Wadd might still make it out of this alive, and he

knew that the other ship was valuable. There was an AI on it, and if he could find the AI core he'd be rich.

Wadd hadn't started out as a mercenary. Yofu mercenaries were rare. Their hands didn't fit guns very well, and they were generally pretty fragile. Not Luvendi-fragile, but not Brakalons either. So Wadd had started out as an electronics thief, which was something his double thumbs helped with a lot.

Now he served as a sometimes-mercenary, sometimes-technical-support employee on the ship. He liked his captain well enough, just not enough to die for him.

He tossed a small device through the airlock door and waited for a few seconds. Once released, the device would start playing havoc with the surveillance systems of the ship. He'd heard impressive things about this AI, and he wasn't about to give it a chance to sound the alarm.

Once he was sure it had gone off, he crept through the airlock tunnel and into the *Shinigami*.

He nearly had heart failure. He would have sworn there was no one in this corridor before, but now there was a woman with black hair and pale skin. And, well, Wadd didn't know much about humans, but this one looked *terrifying*—

The image fuzzed and disappeared.

A hologram.

Wadd smiled. The ship was trying to fight back, but he was going to win this one.

Barna—someone—steal—

Barnabas swore. He had just reached the bridge and was beginning the task of hotwiring the doors open. Apparently, having realized that they could not vent the ship, the bridge crew had locked themselves inside and were hoping he would go away.

Idiots.

Shinigami. Shinigami, are you all right?

Gar's voice spoke in his ear, barely a breath of sound. "Barnabas, there's someone on the ship. I think they're trying to steal it. He's done something to the systems. I'll take care of it."

Barnabas considered this. "Are you sure?" he asked finally.

"Take care of Fedden," Gar assured him quietly. "I'll handle this."

Barnabas paused, conflicted. On the one hand, he did not want to pit Gar against a seasoned mercenary, but on the other, Gar had not asked him to come back. Whatever was going on, Gar was prepared to try to handle it.

He would take care of this as quickly as he could and then get back.

A thought came to him and he used the intercom system in the ship to open a line to the bridge.

"Fedden."

Silence.

"You do not have to speak," Barnabas told him. "Your silence, your speech, your action, your inaction—they do not change what is coming."

Still Fedden said nothing. Barnabas heard him shift in his chair, but he did not speak.

"I have spent long years as an Empress' Ranger," Barnabas told him, "And always I sought *understanding* on the part of those who violated her laws. I wanted all, even those beyond redemption, to understand their crimes before they died."

He thought back over the years. He had few regrets—but some, yes, on this score.

"You have shown me how wrong I was, Fedden. I believed that it was my duty to find an explanation good enough that even those who were beyond atonement could understand their judgment before they passed. It seemed abhorrent to me that someone could be killed without that, but there are those who do not *want* to understand, Fedden. Those like Jutkelon. Like Lan. Like you."

The hacking device Barnabas had placed on the door was getting close to finishing its process. He let out a deep breath and keyed a second command to go at the press of a button.

"Those of you who are here, you were given ample chance to choose another path. You chose this one. Whether you understand the judgment or not..."

The doors slid open. Barnabas tossed a spread of grenades into the room and pressed the button on his wrist to close the door once more. A series of hollow *booms* reverberated through the ship a moment later.

"Does not matter," he finished quietly.

He went to take care of the last mercenary.

26

"Shall we, Kemosabe?" Hirotoshi nodded at her. The mercenaries were still staring at them dumbstruck, as if they had never seen someone get shot before.

They must be the sort of mercenaries who were used to being called in on civilians—people who would just put their hands up and go along with things, not fight back.

Douche-canoes.

Douche-canoes who were about to learn a lesson in manners.

A very, *very* brief lesson.

"I've already got one in the bank." Tabitha jerked her head at Rald's body. "Shouldn't you be catching up? Because I've thought of another forfeit. Whoever loses has to buy sandwiches for everyone else."

"We have so much money that such a forfeit is meaningless." Ryu leapt lightly into the air and his sword flashed as he cut down one, two, then three of the mercenaries in front of them. He looked down at Tabitha with a smile.

"However, I would like to point out that you are no longer winning."

"Jackass!" Tabitha pulled out her Jean Dukes Special and took down eight more mercenaries as fast as she could fire. "Now I am, you—"

The mercenaries finally found their balls and rushed at them.

"Finally. Now, remember," Tabitha called to the Tontos as they all launched into action, "the vengeful ones might be going for Elisa." She threw up an arm to clothesline one of the mercenaries rushing past her and brought her pistol down on his head with a thick crunch. He lay still. "Yep, there goes another one. Hey, good shot," she told Akio, who gave a small bow. A second later she caught sight of another trying to sneak around the main group. "YOU! Mercenary bitch! Nuh-uh! God, this is like whack-a-mole. Anyone have a hammer?"

"I am unfamiliar with 'whack-a-mole.'" Hirotoshi pronounced the term hesitantly. "Does one whack moles with hammers?"

"Yeah!" Tabitha launched herself with a whoop into a group of mercenaries who had decided to mob her.

Their expressions changed from determined to terrified as she bore down on them.

"Oh, did you think that if you attacked *together* you'd get me? WRONG. I'm not surrounded, you've put me in a target-rich environment!" She grabbed two and clunked their heads together like coconuts, then ducked so that a shot meant for her hit one of the mercenaries. "Shooting at me when you've got allies in every direction? You're not very smart, are you, jackass?"

"I object to the use of the term 'jackass,'" Ryu commented. "You called *me* a jackass. Surely I do not deserve to share a name with such terrible warriors. They barely deserve to be fought at all."

Tabitha flashed him a wicked grin. "You can prove you don't deserve to share the name by winning the wager."

"And forcing you to drink Pepsi for a year? You have miscalculated, Kemosabe. None of us want to see your mood should that happen."

"I wouldn't—*ow. Motherfucker*! Listen up, monkey-spunk." Tabitha's foot lashed out and she caught the mercenary who had shot at her in the head twice. "The sole purpose of your life is now to serve as a warning to your friends." She grabbed him by the front of his armor and smashed a fist into his bleeding snout before kicking him in the stomach. The mercenary lay on the ground whimpering.

Tabitha kicked him again for good measure. "What, don't you like that? Aw, is the little human beating up on you? Is it meeeeean? And what were *you* about to do when I showed up?"

"He was about to kill defenseless people," Akio offered dryly as he came to stand beside her. His sword flashed at the corners of her vision as he cleared the area around Tabitha and the mercenaries screamed as they stumbled out of the way.

"Thank you, Akio." Tabitha turned back to the mercenary. "You were about to kill defenseless people. Me hitting you a few times isn't mean at all compared to *that*."

"They...deserved it..." the mercenary gritted out.

"Oh, bad choice." Tabitha kicked him in the groin.

When he didn't give quite the response she expected, she looked at Ryu.

"I believe that the testicles are internal for Shrillexian males," Ryu informed her solemnly.

"Sonofabitch! That's *so* unfair! You mean he was going to kill a bunch of civilians and I can't even give him a swift kick in the balls?"

"Sadly, no."

"Today's your lucky day," Tabitha bitched. "And you don't even know how lucky you are. Because, oh my *God* could I make this hurt if I could just get at your balls."

"They exist," Ryu pointed out. "They're just internal."

"Oh, good point!" Tabitha brightened and shot the mercenary several times. He screamed and went limp. "Not the same effect, but it'll do." She looked around at the other mercenaries. "So what's it going to be, you whale-shit stains? Are you going to run away and make us hunt you down one by one or are you finally going to act like warriors?"

With a roar, they charged as one.

"*Finally,*" Tabitha exclaimed. "Jesus, didn't think I'd be giving a pep talk to mercenaries today."

"I thought it was very inspiring," Akio told her.

"They will die with…" Hirotoshi grimaced as he cut down a couple of the mercenaries. "I cannot even joke about it, Kemosabe. They have no honor whatsoever."

"Focus on the important parts, Hirotoshi. How many have you killed?"

"Twenty-seven," Hirotoshi told her. He whirled, his blade catching another across the chest. "Twenty-eight."

"Fourteen," Akio called.

"Thirty-nine," Ryu answered.

"Ryu's kicking your butts! And mine, actually. I can't allow this." Tabitha took a running leap into the densest part of the crowd. "All right, motherfuckers, it's time to learn some manners! From my Queen directly to your face. Welcome to High Tortuga! Enjoy your fucking stay!"

"We were here before you!" one of them yelled at her.

Tabitha backhanded him and he staggered sideways. "The fuck you were. You were on Devon—a place you thought you ran. You're on High Tortuga now, cupcake, and you are *not* running this show!"

Half the mercenaries found this infuriating and the other half ran. Tabitha and the Tontos went into action with a vengeance, calling out numbers to one another as they took out knots of fighters and chased down the people running away.

A few mercenaries had the bright idea to make a break for the mining town, thinking to do some damage there. Tabitha made sure those died painfully. She flipped through the air and pushed off the wall to land on the dusty road ahead of them and laughed when they skidded to a stop.

"What's the matter, never had your asses whipped by a fine-looking lady before? I hope you don't prefer that as a literal thing, because I have zero intentions of doing it. Yuck!"

She thought she heard Carter laugh as she cut down the mercenaries who had come to the gates and she flashed a smile at those on the wall before heading back into the action.

It wasn't long after that the entire mercenary camp was quiet. Tabitha looked around herself, pleased.

"One hundred twenty-eight," she announced.

"Is that counting all the kills I fed you?" Ryu asked. "One hundred fourteen."

"You're one to talk. You stole six of mine," Akio bitched. "Ninety-seven."

"One hundred thirty-five," Hirotoshi told her with pleasure.

"You're lying," Tabitha accused.

"I would not lie about this." He sounded offended.

"So Akio drinks Pepsi for a year?"

"And buys us all sandwiches," Hirotoshi agreed. "I am looking forward to trying them."

"Much as I hate to say it, before we get sandwiches we should get Elisa to Carter," Tabitha told them.

Akio pointed and Tabitha turned to look over her shoulder. Carter must have been watching when they hid Elisa because he had snuck into the foothills and was now sprinting for her hiding place. As they watched, she came out and ran to meet him.

"Awww," Tabitha cooed. "They're so cute." She frowned. "I wonder where the kids are?"

They headed up the hill to talk to Carter and Elisa. Hirotoshi cleaned his sword as they went.

"I gave you that thingy that cleans it for you," Tabitha groused.

"Taking care of one's weapon is a practice that is both about the weapon and the warrior," Hirotoshi replied, untroubled. "Leaving it in the care of anyone—or anything —else would not be at all proper."

"I got it for you for *Christmas.* Just use it once!"

"Yes, Kemosabe," Hirotoshi acquiesced with the attitude of someone who is preparing to do something very stupid and complain about it for a long time after. "As soon as we get back."

They reached Carter and Elisa, who both had big relieved smiles on their faces.

"Thank you so much," Carter told Tabitha and the Tontos. "I cannot tell you how grateful we are."

"Did she tell you that she managed to sneak most of the way out of the camp?" Tabitha asked, and grinned. "And *then* she stabbed that Shrillexian bastard when he caught her. It was *great.*"

"You killed Rald?" Carter asked Elisa.

"Nooooo," Elisa admitted. "Just the guard at my tent. Tabitha killed Rald. He managed to disarm me."

"Didn't have to do much," Tabitha told him. "Just enough that maybe a sandwich wouldn't go amiss."

"She can't stop eating the sandwiches there and Barnabas drinks the juice all the time, of all things. What do they *put* in the food there?" Akio asked Ryu.

"It's good, whatever it is." Tabitha shook a finger at him. "So don't get them closed down, no matter *what* you might find in the bottles in the basement."

Carter swore softly.

"Oh, yeah," Tabitha told him. "*We know.* We figured it out."

Akio interrupted. "*Barnabas* figured it out. You just—"

"Shut it!" Tabitha glared at him. She turned back to Carter with a smile. "Just be careful not to mix up the bottles when Bethany Anne comes to visit. You don't want that pain. Yeah, I see you getting ready to be all manly and like, 'I could take it.' Nope. You don't want to mess with that shit. She's a fan of saying that pain is an excellent teacher, and you will learn a *shit-ton* if you feed her that devil-stuff."

"Uh-huh." Elisa elbowed Carter. "So shut it."

Carter laughed as he looped an arm around his wife's shoulders. "Point taken. I have to say, though, if I've got one beef with all of you it's that everyone seems to have gotten some shots in but me."

"You run a bar, sweetheart," Elisa told him soothingly. "You'll get some shots in sooner or later."

Carter brightened. "I suppose that's true. Who's up for a round of sandwiches? On the house," he added. "Least I can do."

"Actually, Akio's paying," Tabitha explained. "He did the least work against the mercenaries—"

"The *least* work? You all left me to chase your escapees! I lost time in transit."

"Uh-huh. Nice way to justify your numbers. By the way, should somebody call Barnabas to tell him this is all cleaned up?" A call buzzed on Tabitha's wrist unit and she smiled. "That's probably him now. 'Sup, Big— No, it's an automated message. What—"

She broke off, staring at it.

"What is it?" Hirotoshi asked her quietly.

"We have five gunships inbound," Tabitha told them. "So much for doing this on our own."

"Good afternoon." A falsely-pleasant female voice spoke from their communications devices simultaneously. "Thank you for calling Vigilante Enterprises. We have detected a threat inbound on your position and will be there presently to turn this potential unpleasantness into a beautiful fireworks display. Here at Vigilante Enterprises, we strive to have only the best client experience. To rate this message, press—"

Elisa frowned at Tabitha's hysterical laughter.

"Who is that?"

"Shinigami," Tabitha wheezed. "All right, everyone, let's go find some snacks and sit back to watch the show."

27

Not long before Shinigami's message to Tabitha, Barnabas had gotten back to find an eerily silent ship. Until he saw it devoid of Shinigami's presence, he had not realized how alive she made the place. He could sense that the cameras were not watching him as he walked.

She was either disabled or hiding.

To his surprise, he felt a wave of fury. How *dare* someone come onto this ship and hurt her? He was going to make them pay—but first he was going to turn her back on so she could watch.

It was the least he could do for a friend.

His abilities let him walk near-silently and he went through the familiar corridors with his eyes half-closed, listening for whoever was on the ship.

His ears perked up. There was someone ahead.

You idiot, Gar told himself. You don't have any of the

upgrades yet. You've just been watching some kung fu movies and pretending to be a big-shot. You're going to get yourself killed.

Funny how that wasn't enough to slow him down. He wrapped his long fingers around the pistol and edged through the hallways.

He had heard some screaming echoing strangely through the ship, and some gunshots as well. He had no worries about Barnabas, and the fact that he hadn't come across a veritable massacre told him that no one had done anything *too* stupid.

Yet.

But who the hell was in here? He supposed it made sense for Fedden to have planned the entire thing—get Barnabas off the ship, then have someone steal it.

Perhaps he should call Barnabas back. But no, there were the captives to consider. They couldn't leave Fedden alive.

Gar would have to handle this.

He edged into one of the hallways and heard someone muttering to themselves ahead. The sound was very faint, and Gar froze. If he could hear their voice, they might hear his footsteps. He slipped off his shoes, tucked up his robes, and continued. The pistol in his hands was shaking badly.

His world narrowed to the scope of each footstep. It had to, or he would turn and run. Every instinct was telling him to flee—or throw himself on the person's mercy and say anything, offer whatever knowledge he had, to get them to spare his life. He had been a coward for so long that the habits were ingrained.

I could die here.

Was he ever going to get used to this?

He gritted his teeth and forced himself onward. He was going to *do* this, and what was more, he did *not* intend to die here. He intended to survive this, and—

He came around the corner and saw what the mercenary was doing. He wasn't trying to steal the ship.

He was trying to steal Shinigami herself.

He was fucking furious. The mercenary, a Yofu, was digging around with a series of tools trying to extract Shinigami's AI core from its cradle. Gar could barely think, he was so angry. It was like watching a friend be butchered. He knew what they wanted to do to her, too—they wanted to make her a slave. Until then, she'd be turned off, senseless, alone.

Like *hell* was someone going to do that to his friend.

Gar stepped out into the hallway and walked quickly and quietly up behind the Yofu. *Don't think, don't think, don't think.*

He needed to make sure his shot didn't go into the vulnerable AI core, and he had to do this all in one motion. He couldn't afford to pause and let the mercenary react. He came around the Yofu's side, gun rising, and shot him at point-blank range.

Pain burst up his arms and Gar heard himself scream. Luvendi didn't shoot guns—the recoil was too much for their bones.

Make sure he's dead. You have to be sure. Before he could give himself time to think about the pain that was coming he squeezed the trigger again. He felt the bones fracture, and the world went dark.

He came to not long after. He was in the Pod-doc, its cover open and Barnabas' voice nearby.

"I'm guessing that they knew it would be a tight turnaround," Barnabas was saying, "So they didn't take the time to destroy the colony. It's a small mercy, at least. We'll still want to drop by to bring them the money from the mercenaries, though."

"Already on it," Shinigami reported. Gar, though still dazed, was relieved that she was doing well. "I've arranged to have it partially converted to cash and valuables, which will arrive there soon, and there's also an open account that they can access for the rest of it. That way all their eggs aren't in one basket. Gar is awake, by the way."

Barnabas came into view and Gar smiled slightly. "Hello," he managed. "I don't feel so good."

"We did a fairly quick fix," Barnabas explained. "Your body knitted the bones together very fast with the help of the Pod-doc, so you're going to feel a bit tired. Other than the fractures, however, you sustained no injuries." He smiled as Gar sat up. "You did very well for never having fired a gun before. That was one dead Yofu."

Gar managed a laugh. He could still remember the pain. "I was so angry," he confessed. "I couldn't let him do something like that to Shinigami."

"I'm grateful," Shinigami told him. Her voice softened. "Although I'm a bit embarrassed that I needed to be rescued."

"Everyone needs to be rescued sooner or later," Barnabas told her succinctly. "It's one of the hazards of the job —which, I have to say, Gar is taking to rather better than I expected."

Gar climbed out of the Pod-doc. "It's much easier to be brave for someone else than it is to be brave for yourself."

"Very true," Barnabas agreed. "Thus speaks a vigilante."

There was a pause while Barnabas and Shinigami spoke silently. Gar waited patiently. He was used to the brief pauses in conversation by now.

"We will be upgrading you," Barnabas told Gar. "Shinigami and I are in agreement that if you are to be part of this crew, you should be upgraded enough that you aren't constantly being injured."

Gar could not speak for a moment, he was so touched.

"I would be honored to be a part of the crew," he told them finally.

"Good, then it's settled," Shinigami enthused. "We're thinking we'll give you claws and make it so that you can breathe fire."

"What?"

"Joking, joking. Your face was great, though. By the way, Barnabas, no further word from Tabitha yet. Would you like to send a message?"

"She'd have sent an update if she had one," Barnabas told her. He frowned. "See what you can find from the satellites. I don't want to interrupt her, but I *would* like to know how it's going."

"Give me a few moments." Shinigami worked quickly, muttering to herself in the background as Gar and Barnabas headed toward the bridge.

"You don't *have* to be a part of the crew, you know," Barnabas told Gar. "It's only one possibility. You could stay here for a while doing…whatever you wanted, really."

"I know." Gar shrugged, the latest human movement

he'd unintentionally adopted. "I want to, though. I've had enough of spreadsheets and management. I want to be *doing* things."

Barnabas smiled at him.

Power surged through the ship and they felt the engines kick into high gear. Both of them looked up, worried.

"The initial group of mercenaries is dead," Shinigami reported. "However, someone else must have been keeping tabs on the situation because they're sending gunships—and these aren't any of ours. Someone is determined to make those miners pay."

"I take it you think we can intercept them?" Barnabas' hands had clenched when Shinigami told him what was happening.

"Yep. Sending a message to Tabitha to tell her we're on our way. Everyone strap in—we're going in *hot.*"

2 8

Farfaldri Kat was not foolish.

He had supported the Shrillexian, to a point. After all, a show of force made sense. Allowing the mine events to go unpunished would be bad for business in the long run, and Rald had done a good job of getting support.

On the other hand, Jutkelon's compound was still smoking a month or so later. Kat knew that anyone who could do that, or who could fight dozens of mercenaries on their own, would be more difficult to kill than Rald was anticipating.

Had Rald not paid attention to the stories? This human had not had dozens of allies or a small army. He had taken *on* a small army.

Singlehandedly.

It was clear that Rald was intending to take a large number of mercenaries and charge in headfirst, so Kat simply sent in the hired gunships carrying the guards he'd sent to capture footage, sat back, and waited for the carnage to begin.

Which was how, when that group of humans summarily slaughtered the entire group of mercenaries as he watched in horrified amazement, Kat could put another plan in motion. He called for the gunships to be loaded and move in.

It was impressive, and it was too bad that humans did not seem likely to hire themselves out as mercenaries. They could clearly make their fortunes doing so if they chose.

Humans were notorious for their refusal to submit. However, even humans could not avoid the missiles from five gunships.

Soon this would be over and the point would have been made. Kat smiled thinly and settled back in his chair. This should be a good show.

The *Shinigami* broke atmo with a hollow boom and streaked across the sky toward Tethra. Even with the ship's fake registration, the approach was enough to get the attention of some of the satellites, and Shinigami spent a few moments trading increasingly arcane verification information with the EIs on the other side of the planet.

They were going to make it, but just barely.

Still, Shinigami reflected, that was better than it had been on Banton, where they'd arrived to find the colonists already captured.

She opened a video channel to Tabitha. "Vigilante Enterprises here."

"Hey, Shinigami." Tabitha grinned from the viewscreen. "So when's the fireworks show starting? We've got snacks, we've got... Well, no beer, but we do have fruit juice. It's surprisingly good."

"I *told* you," Barnabas reminded her. "You said I was crazy."

"Yeah, well, I've seen the light now. Anyway, what's the word on the pretty explosions?"

"You'll see them very soon," Shinigami promised. "It's a delicate balance, getting them close enough to be visible but not so close that there's any chance of shrapnel. Still, we at Vigilante Enterprises—"

"Are we really calling ourselves that?" Barnabas interrupted.

"Yes, Vigilante One, we are."

"Are you Vigilante Two?"

"I'm Vigilante Actual. Learn your callsign etiquette. And Gar is our Baby Vigilante, who will someday be a kung fu master."

Gar's cheeks flushed a deep green and he dropped his head into his hands.

"Gar has been watching your movies," Barnabas explained to Tabitha.

"Oh, man. Gar, you and I have to have a movie marathon night." Tabitha held up her cup of fruit juice. "It's gonna be great! And then maybe a night out on the town— get some drinks, beat up some people. I did that with Gabrielle once. It was an awesome night."

"Leave the Baby Vigilante alone," Barnabas scolded her. "You're embarrassing him."

"I hate to interrupt," Shinigami told them, "but it's fireworks o'clock. If everyone would turn their attention to the screens?"

Everyone turned to look. The five gunships came lumbering through the mountain passes. Alien air travel had not always developed along the same lines as it had on Earth, and ships did not need to maintain the same speed as airplanes in order to stay in the air.

These airships had the look of old battered military trucks. Parts of them were rusted, and they creaked and chugged along.

They were full of explosives, however. There was no doubting how effective they would be if they were able to drop those bombs on the mining town.

Shinigami didn't give them the chance to do so. She took aim at the very center of the group as she streaked downward and sent a guided missile into the middle ship.

It exploded spectacularly. The first round of explosions from Shinigami's missile was quickly dwarfed by a second set as the closest munitions went off, and then a third as the fuel tanks and the rest of the munitions exploded.

For a moment, Shinigami waited. She was sure she had seen—

Yes. The ship to the right of her first target exploded along one side and tumbled into the side of a foothill.

"*Hell* yeah!" Tabitha yelled. "*Twofer!*"

The crowd at the mining town cheered and clapped.

The other three gunship pilots attempted evasive maneuvers, but there was no way they could avoid Shinigami's missiles. Three more targeted strikes provided the finale, and only ash was left to rain down on the road.

"You'll also be pleased to know that I located the funding source for these gunships and the Luvendi in charge, one Farfaldri Kat—"

"He's a two-faced sack of shit," Gar interrupted.

"Ah. Well, then I won't feel bad about airing his dirty laundry and sending a couple of pucks his way."

"*Good*," Gar exclaimed.

"All right, I'm going to set us down near the mining town. Everyone hang on."

The news alert pinged on Farfaldri Kat's tablet and he pulled it over to read, curious. He'd made a point to set up alerts in case his name should hit the news, and he saw that it had done so just now. Many times.

His frown deepened.

Then he opened the alerts and his jaw dropped.

Every one of his business dealings under all of his aliases had been posted for the masses to see. He had played rivals against one another, blackmailed business partners, even spent an exorbitant amount wooing the wife of one of his rivals—and it was all public knowledge now.

No. This could not be happening.

His horror was short-lived. When the first puck shattered the window he didn't even have time to scream before it smeared him into paste. He was already dead when a further two pucks smashed into the roof and the building collapsed on his corpse.

Barnabas entered the mining town to cheers.

"Please, no," he protested. "The explosions were all Shinigami's doing, I assure you. And it was Tabitha who helped with the mercenaries." In an undertone to Tabitha, he added, "We really have to do something about all those bodies."

"Eh." Tabitha gave an expressive shrug.

"Barnabas!" Carter jogged over to clasp his hand. "It's good to see you. I don't suppose we could grab a Pod back to Tethra. We've had word that the kids are a-okay. They are probably going to want to live in the Ubuara tunnels forever, actually, but we'd really like to see them."

"Say no more," Barnabas told him. "Elisa isn't badly hurt, is she? We could fix up any injuries aboard the *Shinigami*."

"That would be wonderful." Carter suddenly looked weary. "This was terrifying. I knew that Shrillexian was bad news, but it went wrong faster than I expected. Thank you all for coming to help us," he added to Barnabas, Tabitha, and the Tontos.

"Of course," Barnabas assured him, "We would not let you be hurt."

Carter nodded. He still looked pale and Barnabas understood. They had won a victory, but Carter couldn't help but think what would have happened if Rald had chosen differently—if he'd killed Elisa to make a point instead, or burned down the bar, or any number of unthinkable things.

This was why Barnabas did what he did—to make sure that people like Rald did not continue to hurt people.

"All right, enough depression." Tabitha pointed between them. "It's sandwich time."

"A very good idea." Barnabas smiled at the mining town, which was unscathed. "A very good idea, indeed."

Shinigami's avatar leaned forward to stare at the board, then looked up at Barnabas. "What the hell is this?"

"I assume that's a rhetorical question. It's checkers."

"We play chess."

"We *cheat* at chess," Barnabas corrected solemnly. He made a move. "I assume you've looked up the rules already?"

Shinigami gave him a look and made her move. A moment later, her pieces transformed to look like small grenades. "What?" She put an innocent expression on her avatar's face. "I have to amuse myself somehow, right?"

Barnabas snorted in amusement as he moved a piece.

"You've been quiet lately," Shinigami observed, and made her next move.

"I've been thinking." Barnabas considered, then moved his piece.

"About?"

He smiled slightly. "Something that can't be solved with intellect."

Shinigami made a move. "Do you want to talk about it? This game is garbage, by the way."

"From your displeasure, I can only assume you had a new strategy for cheating laid out." Barnabas studied the avatar, which had conspicuously stopped moving. "Uh-*huh.* I thought so. As regards the issue I have no conclusions, and thus nothing to say yet."

"I hear sometimes it helps simply to talk about things."

"Are you trying to be my therapist?" Barnabas looked at her, bemused.

"I'm *trying* to help," Shinigami retorted. "I don't understand humans all that well, you know."

"I know." Barnabas smiled at her. "And I appreciate it; I do. If it helps, humans don't understand each other too well either."

"I've observed *that* on my own." Shinigami cocked her head to the side. "Gar's waking up in the Pod-doc."

"Let's go look." Barnabas shoved his chair back.

"You don't want to finish the game?"

"Nah, you're right. It's garbage." Barnabas smiled at the avatar as she fell into step with him. "I just wanted to try something new. It's nice having you take corporeal form, or appearing to—although you fuzz out a bit between the projectors."

"Yeah, I don't think my projection capabilities were designed with this in mind."

"Probably not." Barnabas opened the door to the medical suite and let Shinigami precede him in. He saw her smirk. "Yes, I know we can both go through the door at the same time. You look real, though."

"What is 'real?'"

"No philosophy. It's been a long few weeks."

She grinned at him as the Pod-doc slid open. Gar had a smile on his face. He looked taller, Barnabas thought.

"Okay, Shinigami, talk us through the changes."

"Luvendi bone structure *is* comparatively weak," Shinigami began. "My first change was to manipulate the underlying structure to more closely mimic human bones, which necessitated some other changes so that the body would maintain them in their current state. Since they're heavier than Gar is used to, I also increased his muscle mass."

"I feel *great!*" Gar stretched. "So strong!" He held up his hands and wiggled his fingers.

"It's worth noting," Shinigami continued, "that the Luvendi belief in their own weakness has some different causes than you might expect. First, it appears that your diet and lack of exposure to light in early years may have negatively impacted your development, both in bones and muscles. I also detected some organ damage and repaired that. My guess, after subjecting some of your cells to a range of tests, is that Luvendi were meant to have a lot of exposure to strong sunlight, but *not* the type of sunlight you get on Luvendan."

Barnabas and Gar stared at her, fascinated.

"So either something has really changed about the planet—the way the atmosphere filters sunlight, for instance—or your people ended up on Luvendan and lost the records of the migration somehow. My guess would be the latter. You're clearly meant to live near water, so it's probable that they chose Luvendan for that reason, built the towers, and have been suffering the after-effects of living inside and eating a poor diet."

Gar nodded.

"However, what I can find of Luvendi culture suggests that you also avoid physical altercations and stress on the bones as much as possible. I'm guessing that in your formative years your bone structure is highly reactive to impact."

"We've been weakening ourselves," Gar mused.

"It was a self-fulfilling prophecy," Barnabas added, nodding. "Though you wouldn't be the first species to have made horrible choices they thought would be 'healthy.' You should see some of the things humans did over the years."

Gar looked intrigued.

"Anyway, we'll want to fine-tune all this," Shinigami told him, "But the next part of the process will be to begin training for combat and exercise and go from there. Gar, this is *not* going to be comfortable."

"I feel great right now."

"Uh-huh. We'll talk after you've gone through a couple of proper workouts."

"Why don't you go rest," Barnabas suggested to Gar. "Or maybe walk around a bit. Slowly. Get used to your new height."

"Right." Gar headed off. "Thank you, Shinigami."

She grinned. "Can't wait to see you do some real kung fu."

Barnabas rolled his eyes and they left the room as well.

"So where do we go next?" Shinigami asked as they strolled through the corridors.

"Where do *you* want to go?" Barnabas asked. He looked out a window at the curve of the planet below them.

"I want to go smash the main base," Shinigami stated promptly. "I know we wanted to track down the dregs of the whole thing, but since they're holed up and won't be getting any new munitions…" She shrugged and looked at Barnabas, noting his expression. "You've been thinking the same?"

Barnabas smiled tightly. "Yes. My impatience is getting the better of me, I fear."

"Eh, the point of being a vigilante is that you can change your plans on the fly, right?"

"Not…Justice?"

"Oh, right." Shinigami waved a hand airily. "That, too. Where are we going, by the way?"

Barnabas stopped. He had not been paying attention to where he was going and he realized that he had come to the place where he sat alone every day. He went to the window. One of High Tortuga's moons was just visible at the side, looking strangely large given their distance from it.

"Shinigami?"

She waited.

"Do you know my history?" Barnabas asked her.

"Some," Shinigami ventured.

"You know I lost my mind once." Barnabas looked at her.

"You lost someone you loved," Shinigami countered. At the look in Barnabas' eyes, she wished she had not spoken.

"You're correct," Barnabas managed. "So you've heard."

"That's all I know. That's all *anyone* knows, I think."

"Bethany Anne knows more. I… You should as well. All of my story." Barnabas took a seat to stare out at the black. Shinigami had never seen such restraint on his face. In his eyes, she could see a grief that still threatened to swamp him. "It is something that shames me, from the very first piece to the last."

Shinigami chose to say nothing. She could have protested, but there was something in Barnabas' voice that told her that if she interrupted he might not continue to tell the story.

And he needed to.

"To be Nacht in the early days," Barnabas told her, "was to have everything given to you on a silver platter. I do not mean we told people what we were. Michael was very strict; we would never do that. But the family had… resources. It was clear to those who saw us that we were rich and powerful.

"Powerful men in those days were given whatever they wanted. Women threw themselves at me, hoping to become my wife or my mistress. If they didn't give themselves to me, their fathers offered them to me. Sometimes even their husbands did so.

"I took what I wanted and I told myself it was my right. Among my brothers, I alone at that time never believed that my soul had been lost. To my shame, I believed that everything I was given was a gift from Heaven. I believed I deserved it."

His eyes were closed now against the recollection.

"I did good deeds. I often passed small judgments or saved people who needed my help, so I told myself that I was everything I should be. That I was a force for good. In reality, I was self-absorbed. My good deeds were just enough to make me feel that I deserved my wealth. All that changed when I met Catherine."

His voice trembled now. Shinigami felt the useless urge to comfort him but she did not know how to fix Barnabas' pain. What had happened was in the past. She could not change it.

"I saved her from two men who were trying to rape her," Barnabas told her. "It was one of the first acts I had done in decades that was...for more than me. When I first saw her, when she ran past me with them pursuing her, she was like...the dawn, Shinigami. She was pure light and promise. I wanted her to be safe. I killed the men and I spoke into the darkness to tell her I would leave. I was ashamed to be near her. I was death personified, and she was life. For the first time, I saw myself as a human would see me—not simply as a predator, but as a *monster*.

"But she didn't see me that way. She saw the world so differently from everyone else. She had no particular talent for intellectual pursuits. Now, one might say she was not all there. That was part of why I took refuge in my intellect after...everything. I could not bear to be reminded of her."

Shinigami waited, her sense of dread growing.

"She kissed me," Barnabas recalled. There was grief in his eyes, but he was smiling as he stared into space. "I was covered in blood and she came up and kissed me. She loved *completely*, and she loved without reserve. She taught me a way of being that few humans could ever grasp. For many years we were happy together. I told her what I was and she accepted it without question. It did not matter to her.

"And then she got sick. You understand that back in those days, there was none of the medicine there is now, and all my Nacht powers could not save her—except one. She asked me to turn her."

Shinigami's cameras traveled over him, noting the minutiae of his expression; the faint press of his lips, the lines at the corner of his eyes.

"I don't know what else I could have done but try," Barnabas told her softly. "Being turned the way I was, the way Michael was—it was a trial that could break the strongest mind. Nosferatu, the fallen ones, they were the ones who took the respite from the pain and allowed themselves to be tempted. I was afraid Catherine would fail. So many had failed. She just smiled at me and said, 'You will take care of it.' She knew what I would have to do, but she was not afraid. I knew that if I did not try she was going to die. If I did try, she might survive."

Shinigami's avatar nodded.

Barnabas looked down, lost in the memory. "She didn't become Nosferatu, but she wasn't herself anymore either. In some ways, yes. She still took delight in the world, and she still loved me. But she was like a child. She was too trusting, so she had to be watched all the time. One day when I thought she was safe the wrong people found her and—" He broke off. "She died in my arms," he finished finally.

The grief Shinigami saw in Barnabas was overwhelming. Childishly, she did not want to hear what had happened. She did not want to see him in so much pain, but he needed to tell this story.

"I lost my mind with grief." Barnabas looked down at

his hands. "I killed anyone I could find. I wanted to kill them all; that much I remember. I would hunt down whole families and murder them. I was everything I had thought of myself on the night I met Catherine: a monster, death incarnate.

"The only reason that I snapped out of it was that I slipped. I must have; I fell into a river and a branch pinned me. I woke up as the sun was rising and I needed to be more than an animal to find my way out of the trap and survive. So, you see, it was only to save my own life that I came back. Not for anything greater.

"I spent years after that trying to atone, trying to keep it from happening again. I became a monk. I did not believe everything the monks believed, but enough of it was correct. I found some small measure of absolution in hard work and contemplation and serving something larger than myself, but if not for Bethany Anne I would still be hiding from myself."

There was a long silence.

"You said I needed people," Barnabas concluded, "or I would forget why I was doing this. Shinigami, I want to do what's right. I don't want injustice and evil to triumph. But to care deeply for those I save, for friends, for…a lover… I am terrified to walk that path again. I took over three thousand souls when I went mad. I cannot do that again."

Shinigami made the avatar sit next to him. She saw his fear and was touched that he had told her this.

"You won't do it again," she told him. "I believe that."

Barnabas looked down at his hands with a rueful smile.

"I'm serious." Shinigami made the avatar frown. "I *really* believe it. It's been centuries. You're not the same person you were then." She paused. "We won't let you do that again, you know. I believe you wouldn't, but even if you started to go that way, you know we wouldn't let you."

Barnabas nodded.

Shinigami made the avatar stand. Rather than simply flickering out of existence, she made it walk away so he could have the sense of being alone with his thoughts. He was still sad, but she understood that the weight of it wasn't so crushing anymore.

"And don't spend too long wallowing," Shinigami added. She paused at the curve of the corridor and looked back, grinning. "We've got some mercenaries to smash."

Barnabas laughed. "No wallowing, I promise. I'll be there soon."

FINIS

Thank you all for reading *Sentinel*! I am so grateful for the chance to dive back into the Kurtherian universe with Barnabas and Shinigami. Monks in space and a blood-thirsty AI, how can you ask for more?

As always, a thank you to the whole team: Lynne, Steve, the JIT readers, the beta team (Sam, Kim, Jim, James, and Sandy), Jeff, and Eric! You make these books truly shine.

Thank you, of course, to Michael for creating the universe and encouraging so many people to be a part of it, myself included.

Thank you to B, who puts up with all the weirdness of living with an author, and L, who is teaching me so much about the world as he grows up. Even at your teething-est moments, L, you're a wonder!

There's so much coming up this year and next, so I hope you'll take a moment to sign up for the mailing list here to be told about new books and see sneak peeks like excerpts and cover reveals: https://landing.mailerlite.com/webforms/landing/w0k9j4

Head back to the "books by" to check out my other books, including Bellatrix and Risk be Damned set in the KGU, and the Dragon Corps, a whole new universe with stories coming out now!

Happy reading!

-Nat

AUTHOR NOTES - MICHAEL ANDERLE

JUNE 11, 2018

First, THANK YOU for not only reading our second Barnabas and Shinigami story but through to these *Author Notes* as well!

The Kurtherian Gambit grew, and grew, and grew MUCH larger than I had ever suspected it might. Further, I recognized fairly early on that fans enjoyed new characters, so I would often add some to give them a little mental candy in each book.

Like Barnabas.

Unfortunately, the list of fan-favorite characters continued to grow as well. But, I couldn't do a 'Red Wedding' (something George R. R. Martin did, killing off a huge number of the characters) or I'd be eviscerated on the fan pages.

Not something I was willing to risk, and frankly *not willing to do.*

The Kurtherian Gambit isn't about which character dies (like *Walking Dead*) but rather how do they get through the next challenge together, hopefully without a huge battle killing off a few of them?

If you have read the first series, *The Kurtherian Gambit*, you know that there were times that someone died. Part of it was so that I didn't create another (early) 'A' team where five hundred rounds of bullets were used in a firefight, *but no one got hurt.* I did it to keep readers on their toes. It *COULD* happen!

Now we have other series and new characters. Some of those characters are now fan favorites and I scratch my head wondering, "When will all of this end?"

Obviously, not today or tomorrow or this year... Or next year either, I don't think. *The Kurtherian Gambit* is responsible for already creating about fifteen new authors with just the Fans Write project(s), and it looks like the train has left the station without the conductor.

Me.

Speaking of fans, if you are in or around Vegas November 8th, 2018 I'd like to invite you to a huge Author signing event we are having at Sam's town. It's free to get in, just show up – we are going to party like it's 1999.

Check out the website 20booksVegas.com for more info. If we can get at least two hundred to show up this year, the plan is for LMBPN Publishing to throw a WICKED party in 2019.

Because, we are Indie Outlaws, and frankly it's time we party with our friends...All few thousands of them!

Ad Aeternitatem,

Michael Anderle

CONNECT WITH THE AUTHORS

Natalie Grey Social

Email List

https://landing.mailerlite.com/webforms/landing/w0k9j4

Follow Natalie on Amazon

https://www.amazon.com/Natalie-Grey/e/B01MYG7K8P/

Facebook

https://www.facebook.com/Natalie-Grey-393234677682987/

Michael Anderle Social

Website:
http://kurtherianbooks.com/

Email List:
http://kurtherianbooks.com/email-list/

Facebook Here:
https://www.facebook.com/TheKurtherianGambitBooks/